SPINE – CHILLERS

TALES FROM THE WEST

Edited By Tessa Mouat

Years of YoungWriters

First published in Great Britain in 2016 by:

Coltsfoot Drive
Peterborough
PE2 9BF
Telephone: 01733 890066
Website: www.youngwriters.co.uk

FOREWORD

Enter, Reader, if you dare...

For as long as there have been stories there have been ghost stories. Writers have been trying to scare their readers for centuries using just the power of their imagination. For Young Writers' latest competition *Spine-Chillers* we asked pupils to come up with their own spooky tales, but with the tricky twist of using just 100 words!

They rose to the challenge magnificently and this resulting collection of haunting tales will certainly give you the creeps! From friendly ghosts and Halloween adventures to the gruesome and macabre, the young writers in this anthology showcase their creative writing talents.

Here at Young Writers our aim is to encourage creativity and to inspire a love of the written word, so it's great to get such an amazing response, with some absolutely fantastic stories. We will now choose the top 5 authors across the competition, who will each win a Kindle Fire.

I'd like to congratulate all the young authors in *Spine-Chillers - Tales From The West* - I hope this inspires them to continue with their creative writing. And, who knows, maybe we'll be seeing their names alongside Stephen King on the bestseller lists in the future...

Tessa Mouat

CONTENTS

Aldridge School, Walsall

Poppie-Mae O'Grady (12)	1
Shreya Mehta (12)	1
Abigail Taylor	2
Kyle Yip (13)	2
Isabelle Hinks (11)	3
Haroon Afsar (12)	3
Ellan Ashley-Dixon	4
Jasmine Hayden (12)	4
Kalvin Gill (12)	5
Laura Mason (12)	5
Kayleah Bolt (12)	6
Chloe Venables (13)	6
Sophie January (13)	7
Jessica Rose Hall (12)	7
Maryam Iqbal (12)	8
Bethany Gamble (11)	8
James Cox (12)	9
Leah Randell (11)	9
Taryn Cook (11)	10
Lauren Emily Mills	10
Sana Asif (11)	11
Madiha Aftab (12)	11
Lyla Kalra (11)	12
Ellie Davis (12)	12
Maria Ellahi (12)	13
Tamara Howell-Lewis (12)	13
Maisy Garratt	14
Suzannah Warner (12)	14
Abby Shepherd (11)	15
Jasmine Rajania	15
Haseeba Ali (11)	16
Miranda Madziva (13)	16
Teigan Wallace (12)	17
Amelia Watson (12)	17
Jessie Raghunanan	18
Amina Asrar (12)	18
Molly Rutter (12)	19
Mariana Hodgson (12)	19
Amandeep Kaur Sahota (11)	20
Jude Floyd (12)	20
Renée Kaur Samra (12)	21
Ellie-Rose Cogin (12)	21
Deanna Raybe (11)	22

Concord College, Shrewsbury

Iskander Sergazin (14)	23
Robbie Smith (14)	23
Molly Banerjee (13)	24
Archie Oughton (13)	24

Kettlebrook Short Stay School, Tamworth

Liana Cottier (14)	25
Beth Osborne (14)	25
Chenille Reeve (14)	26
Jessica Griffiths (15)	26
Rhys Sandbrook (15)	27
Cameron Bishop	27
Bethany Lewis (14)	28

Nunnery Wood High School, Worcester

Emily Rose Perry (11)	29
Melissa Tout (11)	29
Georgia Bryan (12)	30
Lucy Smith	30
Megan Hughes	31
Amy Pennington (12)	31
Safia Kassim (12)	32

Kirsten Canoy	32	Libby Kermeen (13)	55
Ahmed Bamakhramah (11)	33	Robert Sands (14)	56
Harry James Gilpin (11)	33	James Bradshaw (12)	56
Zoë Hannah Littlewood (12)	34	Milly Cobley (13)	57
Alfie Russell (11)	34	Elliot White	57
Niall O'Kane (12)	35	Shoaib Mohammed (14)	58
Luke Roberts	35	Imogen Pinder-Hampton (12)	58
Esther Lawrence	36	Agnas Linas (12)	59
Omair Iqbal (13)	36	Zoe Ma	59
Mia Silverfield (12)	37	Prithvi Sathyamoorthy Veeran (12)	60
Isaac Shepherd (12)	37	Brandon Colin Norman	60
Katie Smith (12)	38	Harrison (12)	
Max Browning	38	Eleanor Holland	61
Riley Ann Beard (12)	39	Millie Alford (12)	61
Rimsha Akhtar	39	Robert Holmes (12)	62
Charlie Green	40	Jubiya Biju (12)	62
Emily Thomas	40	Asarla Dib	63
Jakub Brydak	41	Ned Deri (12)	63
Ella Ford (12)	41	Erin Claire Lawrence-Bury (14)	64
Alex Gough	42	Rubia Amin	64
Thomas Darby	42	Aniesa Baceva (13)	65
Lucy Evans (12)	43	Reuben Ironside	65
Olivia Neath	43	Victoria Jane Taylor (12)	66
James Thatcher (12)	44	Devon Wills (12)	66
Oscar Bird (12)	44	Isabelle Scarborough	67
Alex Skutt (12)	45	Bobbie-Jo Stedman (11)	67
Matthew Palmer (12)	45	Jago Fortey (12)	68
Joe Evans (12)	46	Jack Beaman	68
Amy Dale	46	Emmanuel Adesola (12)	69
Ibrahim Ali Mahmood (12)	47	Benjamin Allen	69
Hannah Warson (11)	47	James Palser (12)	70
Ethan McDonald-Smith	48	Emer Hancock	70
Emily Maiden (14)	48	Issy Sawyer (14)	71
Lloyd Rawles	49	Eliot Turner (13)	71
Destiny Violet Harborne (11)	49	Molly Ford (13)	72
Imogen Ford (12)	50	Cortni Lamb (12)	72
Chloe Welch (11)	50	Molly Daniels (12)	73
Freya Elizabeth Lawrence (12)	51	Kai Phillip James Steer (13)	73
Millie Louise Yeomans (11)	51	Isabel Hunt (12)	74
Gemma Thomas (12)	52	Kelsey Waters (12)	74
Charlie Mogg (11)	52	Jasmine Richardson (13)	75
Jacob Broadhurst (12)	53	Nicola Dutson (11)	75
Ryan Moores (12)	53	Amy Adnett	76
Chloe Embley	54	Rebekah Dolphin (12)	76
Amy Joy Johnston	54	Millie McCormick	77
Elliot Dotti (13)	55	Daisy Dixon	77

Nicole Ruff (11)	78	Ryan Simcock (12)	100
Matt Ashwell	78	Zara Zeb (11)	101
Ayaan Siddique (11)	79	Hano Zana Baban (11)	101
Kai Trennan (12)	79	Charlotte Warson (14)	102
Jade Louise Bell (14)	80	Sian Williams (13)	102
Solomon Sony (12)	80	Oliver Daw (13)	103
Rosie Hibbard (13)	81	Aqeel Mahmood (13)	103
Hannah Portman (14)	81	Benjamin Kevin Boreham (11)	104
Luke Blundell (12)	82	Louise Cathryn Church (12)	104
Sana Abdul (11)	82	Owen Page (12)	105
Christine Henn	83	Alanah Levett (12)	105
William Barrie Rogers (11)	83	Callum Coffin	106
Lili Mai Florence Worker-Moore (12)	84	Eleanor Sarah Perry (12)	106
Molly White	84	Theodore John Stanley-Palmer (12)	107
Chloe Morgan Wooding (13)	85		
Lydia Howell (11)	85		

PAULET HIGH SCHOOL, BURTON-ON-TRENT

Mollie Montgomery (12)	86	Ellie Mae Dent (12)	108
Hannah Maddison (11)	86	Thomas Ward (12)	108
Angad Sangha	87	Paige Wileman (12)	109
Grace Morris (12)	87	Nicole Wilson	109
Conor Walter Willam Hope (13)	88	Joshua George Asbury (12)	110
Natalia Okrasa (13)	88	Holly Stinson-Smith (12)	110
Jack David Brooks (13)	89	Catherine Ralph (11)	111
William Rea	89	Jack Fotheringham (12)	111
Chloe Smith (12)	90	Freya Shorthose	112
William Tolley	90	Maria Jones (11)	112
Sam Godby (13)	91	Oliwia Chrzanowska (12)	113
Abigail Tarbuck (12)	91	Scarlett Dyche (12)	113
Jasper Struthers	92	Jade Foster (11)	114
Sarah Smith (12)	92	Megan Grimley (11)	114
Rachelle Davies (12)	93		
Liberty Finch (12)	93		

SUNDORNE SCHOOL AND SPORTS COLLEGE, SHREWSBURY

Luke Reid (13)	94	Jack Powell (11)	115
Sophie Nicole Smith (13)	94	Josh Bousfield (11)	115
Alan Manoharan (12)	95	Sam Harris (11)	116
Crista Edmunds (12)	95	Luke Owen Hale (12)	116
Isra Mahboob	96	Ernie Brown (11)	117
Inga Jackson (14)	96	Brandon Colin Melville (12)	117
Declan Lunn (12)	97	Jacob Caslin	118
Joshua Randle (12)	97		
Jack Clayton (13)	98		
Kyle Anhony Goppy (12)	98		
Catherine Nicol (12)	99		
Jayden Scott (11)	99		
Harvey Ormsby (12)	100		

The Mary Webb School and Science College, Shrewsbury

Xander James Connor (12)	119
Natasha Louise Heath (12)	119
Elisha Davies (13)	120
Courtney Beddow (14)	120
George Garrett (12)	121
Danni Varley (12)	121
James Payne (13)	122
Jessica Shurmer (12)	122
Millie Holloway (12)	123
Ryan Antony James Lloyd (14)	123
Jamie Jones (13)	124
Lois Entwistle (12)	124
Ellie-May Parker (14)	125
Megan Richards (12)	125
Billy Davies (13)	126
Millie Batchelor (13)	126
Beth Head (12)	127
Luke Stevens (14)	127
Robin John Milner (13)	128
Amy Morris (14)	128
Jess Richards (13)	129
Branden Bowen (13)	129
Fin Knight (14)	130
Benjamin Woollaston (14)	130
Skye Davies (13)	131

THE MINI SAGAS

SECRETIVE LIARS

'Meet me in the church graveyard.' He hung up.

It was dark and gloomy, I couldn't see anything. I crept through the forest path, heading slowly for the ancient church. Suddenly, I saw a dark, unusual figure in front of me. 'Ben, is that you?' The figure tiptoed closer towards me. 'Ben, this isn't funny.'

'Who said it's funny?'

'That's not you, Ben, is it?'

'No!'

Anxiously, I snatched my phone out of my pocket, ready to dial 999.

'999, what is your emergency?'

'I need help.'

'Where are you?'

'Winchester church graveyard.'

Silence... He whispered, 'She's gone.'

POPPIE-MAE O'GRADY (12)

Aldridge School, Walsall

GIRL GONE MISSING

The night was foggy. I didn't know where I was. I was about to ask for directions but the neighbourhood looked abandoned. All of a sudden, I saw a light switch on in an old church. 'Help!' My hands were shaking, holding the torch. I reached out to open the door. My heart was beating rapidly and the silence sent shivers down my spine. I slowly crept into the mysterious church. Silence. As I walked inside, it was deserted, cobwebs everywhere. 'Hello?' I called. No one answered. I felt someone breathing on my neck...

SHREYA MEHTA (12)

Aldridge School, Walsall

BUMP IN THE NIGHT

Bump! 'Who's there?' I walked over to the door. 'It's my fault for letting my friends drag me into this crazy house. Now they have disappeared.' *Crash!* 'What was that? If that is you Christopher, it is not very funny. Go away! I'm leaving this mad house.' I rattled the doorknob. 'What, it won't open! Oh no! C'mon, open, open! Annabelle, if this is your idea of a joke, it's not funny! Don't be silly, Lyra, you are letting your imagination run wild, you are just paranoid!' *Bang!* 'Somebody's coming down the stairs.' *Clang!* 'What's that? Oh no...'

ABIGAIL TAYLOR

Aldridge School, Walsall

THE SHADOW

Jack was scared, more than scared, he was petrified. His friends, Luke and Pete, had been captured by the shadow. *Groan!* Jack turned back and forth, side to side. 'Luke, Pete?' *Just carry on walking through the house,* Jack said to himself. A high-pitched scream filled the halls. He stopped. A chill touched his shoulder. He screamed. Jack was dead for sure. Laughter filled his ears. 'Happy birthday!' Jack was in a dining hall with food and cake! 'Sorry about the prank. It was his idea.' The shadow loomed above Jack. He stiffened. The shadow took off the mask... 'Dad!'

KYLE YIP (13)

Aldridge School, Walsall

MY BROTHER

'Detective.' He knew what was happening. 'She's right through there.' He pointed towards the silent room at the end of the bitter corridor. His trembling hand clenched the door handle. He walked in. He saw a girl at a table. He joined her. A tape recorder lay next to him. He began to record. 'The twenty-ninth of March 2006, Allicia White, aged fourteen. Victim was found, three stab wounds, two in the neck, one in the left shoulder. She was found near the...'
'I killed him... my brother!' She began to cry.
The detective trembled: 'But... he was my brother!'

ISABELLE HINKS (11)
Aldridge School, Walsall

JEFF

'Argh!' A silent scream escaped the dry lips of an extremely confused boy. His forehead shimmered with glistening sweat as sharp, choking breaths erupted from his lungs. His ears exploded with the sound of his drum-like heartbeat, *dum-dum, dum-dum.* Droplets of transparent tears trickled down his icy cheeks. Wait. Icy? Didn't his body feel like an ember of fire a minute ago? *Creak!* An ominous sound reverberated around his room. His terrified eyes reached the walls covered with a veil of ebony darkness. You could hear the droplets of sweat run down his back. He stared. It stared...

HAROON AFSAR (12)
Aldridge School, Walsall

THE HOUSE

The gnarled trees snapped in the eerie forest and all that could be seen was an old, wooden house. Tom and Kyle walked in cautiously, refraining from making a single sound. 'Hello? Is anybody there?' asked a terrified Kyle. The old, rusted door slammed shut, making the two boys jump with fright. Reluctantly, the friends continued through the house to try and find somebody, anybody. There was a sudden creak of the floorboards, there was just one question rushing through their heads. *Who made that noise?* A shadowy figure came out of the darkness. The petrified boys mumbled, 'You!'

ELLAN ASHLEY-DIXON
Aldridge School, Walsall

HALLUCINATIONS MAYBE?

Why am I here? I'm walking through a cold, damp, spiderweb-filled hallway. An old, dusty door lies ahead of me. 'Hello?' I call. 'Where am I?'
'You're home!' comes a mysterious voice. Screams and laughter fill the room. There are footsteps from behind me. I turn but there's no one there! The shattered window starts to steam up! The door handle is twisting madly. 'This is it!' I whisper. Everything gets louder and closer. I just sit in the corner praying for a miracle. It doesn't come. A big, cold hand grabs me! 'Help!'

JASMINE HAYDEN (12)
Aldridge School, Walsall

GHOSTS?

'Aaargh!' A blood-curdling scream came from the abandoned house. *Thud!* Blood leaked from under the door. Silence filled the house. We all hid behind trees as a girl's dead body floated into the midnight sky. I needed to check it out. Sneaking carefully, I climbed into the not-so-abandoned house through the window. I felt air upon me. The hairs on my back shot up. I was petrified! I froze, shivering. I couldn't move. Would I die today? I couldn't die on my birthday! Suddenly, lights emerged from the darkness. 'Oh my goodness, there's ghosts!'

KALVIN GILL (12)
Aldridge School, Walsall

COMING UP THE STAIRS AFTER A DREADFUL DARE!

Fester crept through the dreary, cobweb-encased hallways of the ancient, abandoned house. Paintings of dolls, clowns and teddy bears eyed her every movement. The terrified feeling of being watched lingered within her and her legs trembled with every step she took. She stopped dead. Slow, heavy footsteps were trudging up the stairs towards her. She carefully twisted the doorknob of the closest room and hid in the corner of it. A human-sized clown sat in the corner opposite and smiled creepily at her. The door leading towards the hallway slowly creaked open. A figure entered...

LAURA MASON (12)
Aldridge School, Walsall

A Place That I Used To Know

The creepy, old, rusty door swung open. The dust invades the place, transforming it. Emily and I entered cautiously. A loud, unwelcoming laugh filled the whole room. It sounded like... no! It couldn't be. I trembled inside. I couldn't speak, couldn't even whimper. Emily was gone! I couldn't move! I finally found the courage to speak out. 'Emily?' Two silhouettes approached me. I remained, calling out, 'Emily?' She was nowhere to be seen. The shadows kept approaching. I didn't recognise the shapes. Then, I knew what it was! It was...

Kayleah Bolt (12)
Aldridge School, Walsall

The Thing

It was there. It unsettled me. I ran. Cold beneath my feet, fog crept in. I had to get out. 'Help!' No reply. The whisper of the trees surrounded me. A house in the distance appeared in view. My legs carried me towards the abandoned wasteland. As I stepped onto the broken, unfixed stairs, I realised that this was my only hope. *Knock, knock!* No answer. I slowly turned the door handle. The door opened with a creak. I stepped into the lifeless shadows that awaited me. *Bang!* The door shut behind me. 'Hello? Hello?' Then, suddenly...

Chloe Venables (13)
Aldridge School, Walsall

THE BASEMENT - THE TRUE ACCOUNT OF 01/01/16

Uncertainty filled me. I was abandoned by Lizy in this basement. It smelt odd and looked creepy, but at least there was a light. I began searching for clues in the piles of paper on the floor. Floorboards above me creaked. *It's just Lizy,* I thought. It continued. The windows forcefully flew open, letting in a harsh gust. It was a warning... 'Get out or else!' But I was overthinking. The light flickered and, with a bang, turned off. I felt a breeze. A cold hand grabbed me. A voice whispered, 'I've got you, there's no escape.'

SOPHIE JANUARY (13)
Aldridge School, Walsall

THE CLOWN

'Daddy!' my stammering voice called out. I thought I'd just wait until Mum came back but I had to find out! 'Where's my dad?' A shiver crept down my spine. I then crept towards my cosy room and hid under my blanket, not knowing what to do. Then I heard a piercing shout coming from the basement. It sounded like an animal. I crept down the hallway and opened the creaking door to the basement. I crept down the stairs. It was my dad. He had a ripped, bloody face and a red Afro...
'Daddy's home!' he growled ferociously.

JESSICA ROSE HALL (12)
Aldridge School, Walsall

WHO IS IT?

It was a dark and stormy night. As Ella sat waiting for her mother, she watched the raindrops fall to the ground. She thought she saw a mysterious black figure. It glanced up at her and disappeared. *Who is he?* she thought. Suddenly, the door creaked open. She looked back to see... nothing. By now she was trembling all over. She reached out for her phone. An icy-cold hand was placed on her shoulder. Slowly, she tilted her head and screamed.

'Darling, what's wrong?' When she saw her mother, she collapsed into her safe arms.

MARYAM IQBAL (12)

Aldridge School, Walsall

RUMOUR OR REAL?

I gradually drifted towards the handle of the deserted house, resting my trembling hand on it. I nudged it down, beginning to ask myself what was on the other side. The door squeaked painfully. I had to go in... Cobwebs lurked across the ceiling. I stepped forward... the floorboards moaned as I went. A weird, black shadow whizzed past my eyes. Was I imagining things or was it real? Shadow or person? *Bang!* I needed assistance. Fast. Beads of sweat flooded across my face. I was terrified. I was petrified. Most of all, I was definitely trapped...

BETHANY GAMBLE (11)

Aldridge School, Walsall

THE MYSTERY

He ran. On and on. He tried to scream for help, but no words came out. He sprinted around every corner and bend, expecting to see something that he didn't want to see. *Where is everyone?* he thought. He felt like crying. He couldn't go on for much longer like this. 'Leave me be!' he screeched. Nothing. Fog was crawling in from every direction as if it had joined the other side. He was all alone. He looked around him expectantly, for something or someone. Through the heavily layered fog, he saw two red, malicious, glaring eyes...

JAMES COX (12)
Aldridge School, Walsall

DRAGGED BACKWARDS

It was a bright morning. The church doors opened and kids bundled in, pulling at their parents' arms. Everyone was excited for the Easter service. Such a happy sight...
Years later, has it all changed? I wandered in. I could hear my heavy breathing as I ventured inside. I was surrounded by moss dangling from the windows. The long corridor loomed in front of me, welcoming my every step. Spiderwebs adorned the walls. An icy-cold hand touched my back, sending shivers down my spine. They dragged me backwards. My last sound was a scream...

LEAH RANDELL (11)
Aldridge School, Walsall

LURKERS IN THE PARK

She had jumped over the iron railings, she was in the park. It was an old theme park that had been deserted twenty years ago due to reports of paranormal activity. The pouring rain made her dash towards the ruined carousel. Over the years, it had lost several horses which now lay broken on the muddy ground. From under the carousel's canopy, Maisy could see that half of the Ferris wheel's capsules had fallen off. When she looked closer, she saw a tall, thin figure in the highest capsule. She screamed. It turned, saw her and disappeared...

TARYN COOK (11)

Aldridge School, Walsall

THE TRAP

The air breathed down my shivering spine as I stepped into the immense cave. A red light shone brightly in the distance. Intrigued, I followed it. My footsteps echoed, making me more fearful than I already was. I'd reached a dead end. *Where has the light gone?* I wondered. Suddenly, from the corner of my eye, I caught a glimpse of a shadowy figure. A figure I'd seen before. I realised it was a trap and I'd fallen for it. I'd been hypnotised. The distorted figure approached me. I heard a blood-curdling scream... my scream!

LAUREN EMILY MILLS

Aldridge School, Walsall

The Kraken

Tina walked through the forest, her body shivering, teeth shattering, legs buckling, tummy swirling. She knew somebody was watching her. It wasn't a person, it was a shadow. Step by step, she felt that she wasn't alone, something was watching her, waiting to outrun her. It moved tree by tree as quick as lightning. *Crack!* It had stepped on a twig and quickly jumped to the top of a tree. Tina looked back and thought her mind was playing tricks on her. What was this scary thing? Would it get to her before she could finally escape?

Sana Asif (11)
Aldridge School, Walsall

Scary, Shattered And Smashed Secrets...

The wind was howling as I stepped into the abandoned house. Suddenly, a tennis ball came out of nowhere and the window smashed, shattering into shards. I went over to look. The bedroom door creaked open. Creepy cobwebs climbed up the remains of the bedroom. *Bang!* A picture in a frame fell on the floor and I picked it up, my hands trembling. There was a photo of a young boy as a farmer. I saw something in the reflection of the picture... droplets of thick blood trickled down my forehead. I looked up... *'Aarrgghh!'*

Madiha Aftab (12)
Aldridge School, Walsall

JOURNEY TO HELL

I was still following the faded pebble trail. I came to a sudden halt. There was one pebble missing, almost like someone wanted me to stop there. My eyes focused on the abandoned bell church. I approached it. The sound I feared the most surrounded me. Silence! Suddenly, the bell struck, everything went into slow motion. An opaque silhouette screamed deafeningly into my ear. I saw red, my ears still ringing. Many distorted figures crowded around me. I felt like I was sinking into a burning black hole. Then I realised I was going to Hell.

LYLA KALRA (11)
Aldridge School, Walsall

THE MYSTERIOUS FIGURE

As she placed her trembling hand on the door handle, a mysteriously dressed figure ran past her. When she turned around, she was met with nothing but the trees. She heaved the wooden door open. As the door slammed behind her, the mysterious figure pounced again. This time, the girl noticed and followed it. Walking through the corridors, she was surrounded by cobwebs. When she turned the corner, the figure was nowhere to be seen. The sound of him led her to the figure. Opening the door, she couldn't believe who was before her...

ELLIE DAVIS (12)
Aldridge School, Walsall

The Frightening Forest

Silence... silence... silence. *Roaaaaaaar!* I looked behind me, to my left, to my right... there was nothing there. I was alone. I went searching and searching for food but there was no hope. *Roaaaaaar!* There it was again. I looked behind me, to the left, to the right. Still there was nothing there. Then I found it, I'd found... food! The ripe, juicy fruit hung from the trees. *Roaaaaaar!* I looked behind me. I looked to the left, to the right, there it was! A distorted figure revealed itself...

Maria Ellahi (12)
Aldridge School, Walsall

The Doll

A shiver trembled down my spine as I passed the gloomy house. It had never intrigued me before. My eyes focused on the house, making me oblivious to who or what was watching me. Before I knew it, I was following a faint, 'Tamara!' that got louder progressively. As I walked down the abandoned corridor, all I heard was the tick-tock of the weathered grandfather clock. The corner led into a child's bedroom. A small porcelain doll was sat, rocking in a chair. In the blink of an eye, I was face-to-face with a living doll...

Tamara Howell-Lewis (12)
Aldridge School, Walsall

THE GUNSHOT

My friends and I walked up to the tall, abandoned house. They pushed me into the door and it creaked open. I stumbled inside and the door slammed shut behind me. A loud, echoing scream filled the air. 'Taryn! Lauren! Jake! Louis!' I bellowed, hoping that it wasn't them. I was trembling, wondering whether to carry on walking. I did. *Bang!* A gunshot fired and I screamed. I thought it was going to be fun, I thought my friends and I would have a laugh, but then I saw it, I saw the one thing I would never forget...

MAISY GARRATT

Aldridge School, Walsall

THE WAY THE WOODS WORK

You always hear fairy tales about princesses who get lost in forests and think that it's the end. But then they get saved by a dashing prince and live happily ever after in a beautiful castle. I was no 'dainty' princess. There was no 'dashing' prince and there was definitely no happily ever after. The cold air was seeping into my body like water to a sponge. I was cold and alone. I called out for what felt like the one hundredth time, once more to hear... nothing. This was it. I was alone and dying in the wood.

SUZANNAH WARNER (12)

Aldridge School, Walsall

THE BEAST WITHIN

The night was cold and eerie as Madeline wandered through the forgotten forest. The trees seemed to scratch and claw at her feet. Suddenly, out of nowhere, a stone-cold church appeared, sending a cold shiver down her spine. As she opened the rusty hinged door, she was met with a mirror. Staring back at her was one of the most flea-ridden creatures she had ever seen. Her heart began to race. She reached a trembling hand towards the mirror and was surprised to find that her hand went straight through. It felt like her own...

ABBY SHEPHERD (11)
Aldridge School, Walsall

THE DARK NIGHT

The night was pitch-black. The strong wind was bitter. I was frozen. I scurried through the piles of damp, rotting leaves, hoping the end of the forest was close. Deep down, I knew I was wrong. The cold breeze pierced my skin as my thoughts drifted to the surrounding noises. Was I being followed? I convinced myself it was just my mind playing tricks on me. Even then, I was still terrified. That was when I saw it, standing there, staring at me. I hesitated but then took another terrified step, not knowing it would be my last...

JASMINE RAJANIA
Aldridge School, Walsall

BENEATH MY FEET

Beautiful trees used to glisten as the solemn singing spread through the church. *Bang!* It had now turned into a dismal cemetery. Many souls haunted, the bodies long forgotten, deep within Hell. Whilst searching for my father's grave, I could sense something wrong. I picked up my pace and stumbled. A bead of sweat trickled down. I saw a coffin. As I turned back, I heard a creak. The coffin opened, the body had vanished! More sweat trickled down me. Just then, a cold hand reached out for me. 'Aaarrgghh!'

HASEEBA ALI (11)
Aldridge School, Walsall

CHASE

Panting, I raced through the thick mist, my steps crunching the autumn leaves on the forest floor. The icy breeze slithered down my back and the tips of my fingers. Becoming confused by the maze of trees, my eyesight doubled. I hopelessly staggered past the lurking trees that seemed to sway to the rhythm of my rapid heartbeat. The shadows crept nearer and faster than ever. I stopped. My ears prickled as I heard the sudden rustle of branches. A feeling of enclosure fell upon me and that was when I knew it was the end...

MIRANDA MADZIVA (13)
Aldridge School, Walsall

MYSTERIOUS FIGURES

I was jogging over to my friend's house when a black figure caught my eye. 'I'm sure it just went into that house!' I walked over to the house and knocked on the door. As it opened, it slammed behind my back. I crept through the corridors. Suddenly, I spotted a small, drooping figure on an old rocking chair. I tiptoed over to find it was a small boy. He looked up at me with a pale face. Out of nowhere, he started screaming. I ran into a dusty closet. He found me... he was holding a bloody knife.

TEIGAN WALLACE (12)
Aldridge School, Walsall

HELL HAS RISEN...

A blood-curdling scream pierces the air. Composing herself, the screaming instantly stops. The flowers in her hands are long forgotten. The coffin lies in the centre of the yard. Eve sprints to make it to her dead mother's grave. She had died here but Eve believes she still lives. A scraping noise shoots through the atmosphere like a bullet. She turns slowly to see an empty deathbed. Eve freezes. Cold hands grasp her ankles. She spins around to witness thousands more, digging out of Hell. Eve is doomed...

AMELIA WATSON (12)
Aldridge School, Walsall

IN THE WOODS

The night was still and dark. The owls sang their songs. The trees swayed from side to side and shadows covered the path. A loud scream echoed through the trees and footsteps left a trail in the mud. Darkness created an eerie tension and twigs snapped in the distance. Nobody could be seen for miles. The air was cloudy. What could be in the distance? Who could it be? A wooden door swung open and a tall, dark figure walked towards me. His hand reached into his pocket. He pulled something out... oh no!

JESSIE RAGHUNANAN

Aldridge School, Walsall

THE CREEP

I saw the church. It used to be happy and jolly but now it was eerie. The graveyard spirits took over. Something was following me. I had to go in the church, it was my only option. My friend abandoned me. Some friend she was! I ran and ran past the weather-beaten gravestones. I stumbled in. 'Hello?' I yelled. I stood there and felt weird, like someone had walked on my grave. I saw an organ and the Psycho theme started to play. I heard voices, saw shadows. I turned around. 'Holy...'

AMINA ASRAR (12)

Aldridge School, Walsall

THE POWER CUT

The power was down. I had nothing to do other than sit there all alone. The sound of footsteps suddenly came from upstairs. I decided to go up and investigate. My heart was in my mouth. The lights flickered on and off. 'Hello?' Shivers ran down my spine. Before I knew it, I was in darkness. 'Surely there is some source of light I can use to see.' I put my hand out to search. I felt what seemed to be skin. I heard breathing and felt icy breath. I knew that I wasn't alone...

MOLLY RUTTER (12)

Aldridge School, Walsall

TAKE ME TO CHURCH

The bell tower chimed two o'clock; no one was around. Nothing to be heard except the screams of a small five-year-old girl. As the fog eerily rolled in, I headed for the church. The door was unlocked. I went in. The screams grew louder and louder. Walking amongst the deserted rows, my blood curdled. The screams came from the next room. I walked to the door. I opened it. Silence... no one was there. Confused, I turned around. As I did, a hand reached out, touching my shoulder...

MARIANA HODGSON (12)

Aldridge School, Walsall

THE APOCALYPSE

Creak! The door slid open and I was lost in time. I saw it, the end of the world. I always knew it would happen, now it wasn't going to stop! I saw it, a group of people and they all had the same logo on their shirts. What did it mean? Suddenly, I realised... the apocalypse had come. Then someone slowly reached out to touch me...
I woke up. It was only a dream! Then, I saw it all. A cold shiver ran down my spine. I realised it wasn't a dream...

AMANDEEP KAUR SAHOTA (11)

Aldridge School, Walsall

RUNNING BLIND

The further she ran into the forest, the closer to her it got. She couldn't see it, the midnight made sure of that. Though because of the unearthly screaming, she knew it was already closer! Tripping over vines and logs only gave it a leg up. Trees got more compact and vines seemed to be growing dramatically fast, almost reaching out towards her. It grabbed her leg and she fell onto a log.
She woke up in a box... a coffin.

JUDE FLOYD (12)

Aldridge School, Walsall

STRANGER DANGER!

The cold breath. My hair on end. Frozen in time. Who's holding the gun to my head? On a dark, gloomy night in a desolate house, I stood there as cold as ice. The tornado was engulfing the houses and this was the only one left. Would that be the cause of my death? That brings me back to now. A trigger has just been pulled. The distorted figure appears out of nowhere. *Bang!* The shot is fired... Now what will cause my death?

RENÉE KAUR SAMRA (12)

Aldridge School, Walsall

ELIZABETH AND THE APOCALYPSE

It has been six days since it started. Being chased all day and night isn't easy you know. My mother has been gone for four days now. I saw her being ripped into tiny pieces by the walkers. I slowly crept into a giant crowd of them yesterday. She was there. Her young, beautiful face had gone, turned into a horrible, bloody mess! I tried to keep the tears in, but I just couldn't. It started, they came for me...

ELLIE-ROSE COGIN (12)

Aldridge School, Walsall

QUESTIONS

Where was I? What was I doing there? How did I get there? These were questions that remained unanswered. I decided to stop worrying. I saw many craters and holes in the gravel. I then questioned myself again. What happened here? All I knew was that this wasn't going to be easy, especially for me. I wondered, *Will anyone find me here?*

DEANNA RAYBE (11)

Aldridge School, Walsall

BEHIND THE DOOR

At 3am I was woken up by something. Quickly running into the corridor of the house, stopping every two or three seconds, then a following silence. My room was at the end of the corridor. The walls weren't soundproof, you could hear everything. It was approaching, closer to my door. I could now feel it behind my old, wooden door, breathing heavily. A gentle, quiet scratching got louder, growing into an alien thump. I closed my eyes and repeated, 'The door's locked. Calm down.' Slowly, I opened my eyes, realising the door was wide open...

ISKANDER SERGAZIN (14)
Concord College, Shrewsbury

THE ESCAPEE

Silence. Nothing but deafening silence. Breathing heavily, I take in my surroundings. A deep, dense and dark forest is all I can see. Tall, thin pine trees rise from the ground like the world's tallest gravestone. For the first time in three days, I feel happy with what I'm seeing, as my current location tells me that I have put enough distance between myself and... that place. I set off north, again, alone. Or so I think. At that moment, I hear footsteps. They aren't mine. I run... trip... fall. Then nothing...

ROBBIE SMITH (14)
Concord College, Shrewsbury

THE NOISE

I heard a knocking at my door. Who could be visiting at this time of night? I went to the door, nothing was there. I went to bed and the noise started again. In a fit of rage, I stormed outside, expecting a group of children playing knock and run. I tried to get back to sleep again. However, the banging noise haunted me all night long. It got into my head. It made me turn in my bed. It made me shiver.

The next morning, I opened my wardrobe to find a man banging on my closet wall.

MOLLY BANERJEE (13)

Concord College, Shrewsbury

IT

It was dark, misty, cold. There was a slight breeze in the air. I could hear a faint rustling noise behind me. I attributed it to the wind in the trees. Something moved and I looked for it. There was nothing there. I felt it again. Then, *thud, thud, thud!* Something moved past me. I felt the wind go down my back. The wind had ceased. The last thing I heard was, 'Time runs out.'

ARCHIE OUGHTON (13)

Concord College, Shrewsbury

INK BLOOD

Black. Black shrouded me. It filled my lungs... this sinister, dense substance crawled inside every crevice, in and out of my body. I gasped for breath, my eyes and chest pulsating in agony, radiating light. I regained my memories of what just happened. Infinite voices, demons and children started ascending from everywhere, foreign taunting, the confusion of what happened, my mind fell to ruins. The book, the ink, seeping into my skin from that final page. Guilt. Fear. The sensation of artificial, forced emotions. Amongst the noise, I heard 'Apicen Inferno' and the darkness dispersed.

LIANA COTTIER (14)

Kettlebrook Short Stay School, Tamworth

THE DARKNESS!

She walked through the dark, misty woods. She heard a screeching sound. When she looked around, there was no one there. Cautiously, she walked deeper into the woods. It got louder and louder until she saw a tall, skinny man standing behind a tree. She stood there like a statue. She was shocked at what she was seeing. There was no face! He advanced in a menacing way... the figure struck terror through her heart. She withered into the undergrowth. Her mouth opened. No sound. She felt her soul fading away. Her knees buckled. She slumped to the ground... darkness!

BETH OSBORNE (14)

Kettlebrook Short Stay School, Tamworth

THE FACTORY

Bang! A gunshot sounded throughout the village. But where did it come from? The police were informed about the sound. Two days later, they discovered that a 14-year-old girl was missing. The police on the case were strong, fierce, scary and determined to find the girl. They found an old, ruined building... a meat factory. They walked in and saw a knife covered in blood. Carefully, they followed the trail to a grim, solid door... a freezer. They found a girl in the freezer. It was the missing 14-year-old. It was just the beginning...

CHENILLE REEVE (14)

Kettlebrook Short Stay School, Tamworth

THE TORTURE

'Argh!' I heard shooting. My head whirled towards the sound. Should I go and see what was happening? I started to open the door. I heard a man whisper, 'Help me!' I barged through the door. I couldn't believe what I saw... a man hanging by giant fish hooks in his shoulders. I heard people coming into the house. No time! No chance to save him! Save myself! I ran towards a window. It wouldn't budge. Frantic fingers fumbled. My life was in my own hands. I turned as the noise increased. My face froze. My time had come...

JESSICA GRIFFITHS (15)

Kettlebrook Short Stay School, Tamworth

The Asylum

The night was dark, clouds hovered in front of the moon, wolves howled in the distance. There lay an abandoned building. We crept closer. Jim and I looked at each other as we got closer to the building. Staring at the floor, we saw a sign. Quickly brushing the mud off the sign, it said: *Cloverfield Asylum.* Upon reaching the door, shivers went down my spine. We opened the door and slowly walked in. The door slammed, sending the room into darkness. Using our torches to guide us, we crept in. There was a loud bang. I turned around...

Rhys Sandbrook (15)
Kettlebrook Short Stay School, Tamworth

Ghost Town

I can see an old apartment building, seemingly unused. I'm running for it. I still feel watched, chased. I look frantically for an unlocked door as I hear someone coming up the stairs beside me. I find one. I run in quickly and move the sofa in front of the door. As he tries to knock the door down, I look for a weapon. All I can find is a butter knife, hardly enough to defend myself. I hide in the bedroom closet. He's in. He's walking closer. I'm frozen. He knows where I am. He sees me. Please, no!

Cameron Bishop
Kettlebrook Short Stay School, Tamworth

RUNNING

Running for my life. Running so fast I could hear the wind in my ears and my heart beating in my chest. I couldn't run much longer. I used my last ounce of energy and hid behind an oak tree. Everything was quiet. I took a chance and looked out from behind my hiding place. Nothing there. I was in a graveyard. I stepped out from behind the tree and walked between the decaying gravestones. I had a feeling I would be joining them soon. There was a noise behind me. I was running again...

BETHANY LEWIS (14)

Kettlebrook Short Stay School, Tamworth

THE CALL FROM HELL

Jane was in town, a phone rang in her pocket - Jane didn't bring her phone. Curious, she answered it.

'Hello Jane.'

'Who's this?'

'Loopy-loo.'

'Louise? But you're dead!'

'I am, I'm calling from Hell.'

'I'm calling the police!'

'Who else knows the nickname you gave me when you bullied me?'

'This seems alien, what's Hell like?'

'You'll find out soon!'

'How will I find out?'

'I promised I would get revenge.' Louise let out a spine-chilling cackle.

Jane stepped into the road. A driverless car careered towards her.

A blood-curdling scream. A crash as metal hit skin.

EMILY ROSE PERRY (11)
Nunnery Wood High School, Worcester

THE DOOM DARK WOODS

There was a little boy playing football. Then, accidentally, he kicked the ball in the dark, daring woods. Music was playing, bouncing on the deadly trees. He was frightened! He screamed like a werewolf! He sprinted like a cheetah. Eventually, the boy got home. But when he looked in the mirror, it was not his face...

MELISSA TOUT (11)
Nunnery Wood High School, Worcester

LISA

Ding-dong! 'Emily, there is a package for you.'
Emily opened the box. 'Oh, it's a doll.'
'Go play with her then,' said Tiffany.
That night, Lisa the doll came alive and ran across the bedroom floor. 'Hello, I'm not going to hurt you. My name is Lisa, what's yours?'
'Emily!' cried the little girl.
'Wanna help me kill?'
'Um, OK, I guess,' said Emily.
Lisa did a voodoo chant. 'Awaken the dead souls,' said Lisa.
Thunder roared outside. Emily took Lisa, grabbed a knife and stabbed her mother. After, Tiffany turned Emily back and killed Lisa.

GEORGIA BRYAN (12)
Nunnery Wood High School, Worcester

THE SILENCE

Night drew in fast. I would never make it home. A church stood tall in the distance. I'd spend the night there. The birds squawked, trees rustled. The door creaked loudly. 'Hello?' I stammered with fear. No reply.
Then, 'Ring-a-ring o' roses.' A ghostly voice echoed around the church. A sudden flash of lightning revealed a doll's face. I was frozen to the spot. 'A pocketful of posies...' She advanced towards me. 'Atishoo, atishoo...' I tried to scream, but couldn't. Why did I come here? 'We all fall down!' I hit the floor. The dreaded, deadly silence...

LUCY SMITH
Nunnery Wood High School, Worcester

Clowning Around

'Eeeegh!' The decrepit, old door swung on its hinges. Two sets of feet appeared out of nowhere. Watching from the window, a crumbling face chuckled.

'Tim!' the little girl called to her brother.

'Yeah?' came her brother's familiar tone.

Swallowing her fears, Bella moved through the deserted joke shop. The moon cast grotesque shadows on the ground. It was cold, chillingly cold. Unnerved, Bella looked at the rows of innocent-faced china dolls. Their eyes followed her.

'Eeheehee!' A jack-in-the-box sprang open. Suddenly, Bella saw a figure appear... grotesque, with a bulbous, red nose. The clown grinned...

Megan Hughes
Nunnery Wood High School, Worcester

Error: Infinite

Liz loves video games; when she found a new game online, she was excited! However, as soon as she clicked download, the world's deadliest virus was unleashed. Her computer immediately flashed a message saying: 'Error: Infinite'. Without warning, her computer switched itself off.

Only a few hours later, every single device she owned was infected. Her phone kept getting messages from 'Infinite', saying stuff like 'There's no escape now...'

One night, her computer switched itself on and a very mysterious killer came out of the computer, making Liz's life a living nightmare for an infinite amount of time...

Amy Pennington (12)
Nunnery Wood High School, Worcester

The Cold, White Hand

On a gloomy, dull day, the sky was as grey as the ash on a cigarette.

'Today, we've decided to visit your grandfather's grave,' Mum emotionally commented. Slowly, I got dressed. 'Tom, let's go!' Mum screamed.

Finally, I grabbed my umbrella and raced to the car. Seconds, minutes, hours passed. Dad commented, 'We're here!' I examined the surroundings, it seemed to be the middle of nowhere. I could hear a pin drop in the vicinity. Abruptly, rain gushed down. 'Place these roses down,' Dad added.

Gingerly, I knelt. *Rumble!* They vanished. A white hand grabbed me. 'Argh!'

Safia Kassim (12)
Nunnery Wood High School, Worcester

Eaten

A blood-curdling scream pierced the eerie silence. We all stopped and stared at each other. 'What was that?' Emily gasped, as she ran from her tent.

'Maybe it was Luke,' Nick laughed as I snarled at him. However, by the look on my sister's face, I knew it was no laughing matter. Then, suddenly, another scream echoed throughout the derelict wood. Then we knew something was wrong. 'Wait, where's Anne and Izzy?' Emily shrieked. We started sprinting through the woods, trying to find them. Nick found a horrible sight, the remains of our dead friends, viciously ripped apart.

Kirsten Canoy
Nunnery Wood High School, Worcester

THE ABANDONED WOOD

There was a haunting wood which, if people entered, they would never be seen again. A group decided to investigate the terrifying wood. As soon as they entered, the atmosphere shook uncontrollably, spine-chillingly. The leaves fell down and dried out. One of the investigators disappeared and suddenly they heard, 'Aarrgghh!'

They were petrified so they ran into the darkness, not realising they were getting closer to the beast's den. They didn't know what their fate would be!

The two remaining investigators heard the blood-curdling cries of their friends, frozen on top of a tree, not knowing if they would survive.

AHMED BAMAKHRAMAH (11)

Nunnery Wood High School, Worcester

GHOSTLY AWAKENING

It's a cold, desolate night, when the misty fog slowly creeps into the eerie cemetery. Moonlight strikes down, creating a gloomy spectrum. The night watchman, Ross, thinks he knows everything that happens in this job, that isn't the case. Ross sits on a rusty bench, thinking nothing will happen, he falls asleep.

Woken by a booming shriek, still drowsy, Ross gets up and looks towards the cemetery. That's when he sees a translucent, ghoulish figure with red symbols glowing around him. The graves rise up and erupt with bodies. A bellowing, rough chant fills the air, 'The dead will rise...'

HARRY JAMES GILPIN (11)

Nunnery Wood High School, Worcester

THE LAB MURDER

Twiglet was different from the rest of the piglets. He wanted to be a scientist. One stormy night, Twiglet trotted upon a large, lonely laboratory. As he stepped onto the dust-covered, creaky floorboards, the door slammed shut behind him. Twiglet was trapped. Nobody was in there, except for huge, green eyes crawling around amongst abandoned science experiments. Twiglet took two steps back, but it was too late. The eyes were after him. He ran frantically, smashing into DNA, poison and other glowing bottles. A tall, dark figure appeared through a suffocating fog. That was the end of little Twiglet.

ZOË HANNAH LITTLEWOOD (12)

Nunnery Wood High School, Worcester

DEAR OH DEER!

News reports of deer acting strangely intrigued but didn't worry Geoff. It turned out he encountered his first buck by slamming into it with the front of his car as it suddenly leapt from a hedgerow.

Approaching the mangled corpse, Geoff noticed a chewed human arm poking from a split in the deer's side. A growling noise came from the trees, focusing his attention. A shiver ran down his spine as three more deer, eyes blazed, fangs gleaming, foam dripping from their muzzles, came lumbering towards him. Geoff felt nauseous with the realisation that things would never be the same...

ALFIE RUSSELL (11)

Nunnery Wood High School, Worcester

THE DEAD WAKES

'Come on, Gus!' yelled Gerald as he dragged his younger brother into the eerie house at the end of the road.

'Why are we exploring this old wreck? I'm telling you, it's full of cobwebs anyway!' replied Gus.

As they entered the building, the air became suddenly cold and dry, as if the life was being sucked out. As they turned to the stairway, they saw a blood-curdling figure. He bellowed, 'Eugene sleep, Eugene walk, Eugene kill!' This was the last that was ever seen of those poor, exploring boys from 57 Waverly Place. That house was never disturbed again.

NIALL O'KANE (12)
Nunnery Wood High School, Worcester

JACK'S UNLUCKY DAY, PART 2

'Can you two get more water?' exclaimed the mother.

'We will in a minute,' answered Jack.

'On the way you can get chocolate,' replied the mum.

'Yay!' shouted Jack and Jill as they ran to the door.

On their journey to get water, Jack and Jill found themselves in a dark, gloomy, mysterious wood in the middle of nowhere. There, staring at them was a broken, crumbling abandoned well. Jack ran up to it. 'I can hear running water. We can get it from here.' Then, he slipped.

'Jack! Are you there? Answer me please!'

LUKE ROBERTS
Nunnery Wood High School, Worcester

THE STORMY SHIPWRECK

Peering ahead, I saw it. The creaking, groaning old galleon lying abandoned in the grey Cornish sea. Vicious rocks bit into her wooden sides. Her ragged sails beat angrily in the chilly breeze. I shivered. I was alone. Venturing out to find this ancient ship was something my friends had refused to do. Moonlight struck the wreck, forming pearly beams that glowed like silver. 'Come closer, come closer!' Were those eerie whispers coming from her? I felt myself pulled forwards until I was wading through the cold, lapping waves. 'Come closer!' My heart raced. A hand clasped my shoulder...

ESTHER LAWRENCE
Nunnery Wood High School, Worcester

TROY THE TALKING TREE

Once upon a time there was a young boy named Nero. He lived in a spooky lair beneath a forest. Nero's life was fine until one night he heard suspicious noises. Nero went to investigate the constant rumble. 'Hello?' shouted Nero.
'Hey!' replied a tree!
'Am I dreaming?' said Nero in shock.
Magic happened that night. Troy, the talking tree, became best friends with Nero. Troy felt like he was being watched. There was someone there. He came for Troy. He was getting closer. *Bang!* It was just a fox! Troy and Nero lived happily ever after!

OMAIR IQBAL (13)
Nunnery Wood High School, Worcester

The Boy In The Painting

Nurseries are meant to be happy places, not like this one... dark, sinister, creepy.

'Hello, I'm Rachel, here to babysit Toby,' she called into silence. There wasn't a trace of human activity. Floorboards creaked underfoot as she went in search of a breathing soul. A rotting wall was home to a haunting painting of a boy. He was said to be dead. The boy was Toby. The babysitter stood, confused. *Bang!* A window slammed violently, demanding to be heard. Rachel swung around in a flash. She was being watched. A hand clasped her neck and yanked her into the frame.

Mia Silverfield (12)
Nunnery Wood High School, Worcester

Eyes Of Fire

Maggie casually strolled home from school. The wind was howling and she was concerned because it was already getting dark at 3pm. Unfortunately, she had to walk through a haunted forest on her way home. With no choice, Maggie entered the desolate trees, hearing faint howling sounds approaching. *Snap!* A huge twig had cracked underfoot as she stumbled to the floor. Getting up swiftly, two fiery red eyes appeared in-line with Maggie's, gleaming and fading every ten seconds. Unable to cope with the confusion and shock she collapsed in a daze. Was it a dream? No, not this time.

Isaac Shepherd (12)
Nunnery Wood High School, Worcester

What's Outside?

A dark, bone-chilling, gloomy night; he turned on my beacon. I'd never seen him before. I'd have recognised his gangly figure, emerald-green eyes, pale-black skin. Usually, I felt alone guiding the ships. John was different.

The wind howled; he got up to look outside. He was nervous. He opened my door, torch on, down my creaky steps he crept until he met the grainy sand. Something breathed on him. Something cold, damp and mysterious. Its teeth were razor blades, eyes red as fire. Moonlight hit its fur. Fur that shimmered like metallic knives. What was it? Who was it? John...

Katie Smith (12)

Nunnery Wood High School, Worcester

The Visitor

The desolate night spread over Birmingham and took a young couple by surprise. They hurried home. 'Finally, we're home!' exclaimed Felix whilst charging inside to regain warmth. His wife, Angeline, begged her husband to lock the door tight. Before he did, a man approached their home. The man stood before them wearing a thick, ebony cloak. He pleaded to stay the night. Unfortunately, they allowed him in. The night soon grew. The couple settled into bed, Felix heard a scream. The screech forced Felix to get up. He suddenly felt something leathery grab his leg! 'Angeline?'

Max Browning

Nunnery Wood High School, Worcester

INTO THE ATTIC

The attic was dingy, overcrowded and bleak; that's why Jensen never went up there - until today, when he was left in his currently uninhabited, decaying house. Swinging the ladder down, he climbed up, wincing at the ear-piercing creak it produced. After unsuccessfully trying to find the lights, Jensen came across a decrepit diary - the title? 'The Ghost of Elm Bank'. He opened the book, but immediately regretted it; out of the pages flew a ghostly white figure that squealed as it turned to face him, its voice eerie as it echoed around the room. 'Thank you... brother...'

RILEY ANN BEARD (12)
Nunnery Wood High School, Worcester

THE CRAZED TEACHER!

'Hello?' The cold sneaked through the windows and into the hall. 'Hello?' He tried again. *Strange,* he thought. He read the text again. 'Meet me at the school'. He walked to the classroom, no one. Suddenly, he heard footsteps. He turned... nothing. *Tap, tap!* He turned, nothing again. *Tap, tap!* He turned, there was the crazed teacher. There it was. He was too scared to move. It came closer and closer but there, in the corner of its lip, he saw a birthmark shaped like a dagger. He grabbed the mask of its face and there it was. 'Mum!'

RIMSHA AKHTAR
Nunnery Wood High School, Worcester

BILLY BEAVERS

Two blood-red eyes beaming with rage and the intent to kill hung in the distant void. The eyes tilted as sparks flew out of the side. He thought he was a master thief, that he could thieve Billy Beaver's mail; he'd be rich. He'd planned something extravagant, he'd go down in history! The figure crept closer as it sang, 'You can run, but you'll trip up.' The figure leapt out... Now there was one more puppet for his master's game, controlled with demented strings for unspeakable crimes. The attractions were once innocent children. Will you join them next... ?

CHARLIE GREEN

Nunnery Wood High School, Worcester

CLAUDIA!

One night, when the snow was heavy, the wind howled loudly. Lucy was babysitting Claudia when she heard a tap, tap on the window. She crept towards it. Slowly opening the curtains, *bang!* There was a note. It read: 'Look behind you'. She spun her head as quick as lightning. There was nothing there. All of a sudden, she saw a face in the mirror! 'Argh!' She rang the police. When they were there, they found no footprints behind where she stood! 'Claudia! Claudia! This isn't funny! You're dead to me now!' But Claudia had been asleep all night!

EMILY THOMAS

Nunnery Wood High School, Worcester

ADVENTURES OF YIKA

Yika was woken up by her grumpy dad who was rich and elderly. He shouted, 'I need to go to the shops, you'll be alone!' Yika was always left alone. Her dad got in his Lamborghini and drove off. To his surprise, he got stuck in traffic... trapped!
Meanwhile, Yika was playing with a bouncy ball that dropped into the dark basement. Yika pulled the light string and went in. *Crack!* The light bulb smashed. The door slammed shut. Yika was stuck! There was no way she could get out. Suddenly, something touched her back and whispered, 'I'm here...'

JAKUB BRYDAK
Nunnery Wood High School, Worcester

GUILTY

Tap! Tap! She woke. The noise was coming from under her bed. No, it wasn't her bed, it was a hospital bed on the 13th floor. The walls were pale and cracked, as were her lips. She was strapped to the bed. Why? A white, wrinkled face slid from under the bed. *Bang! Bang!* He disappeared and reappeared, sitting on the bed, faster than an eye blink. 'It's your entire fault, everything.' No, it was a malfunction wasn't it? The words wrapped around her brain. He faded. Her restraints loosened. She had the urge to go to the window... *Guilty.*

ELLA FORD (12)
Nunnery Wood High School, Worcester

JAMES' GAME

James is a typical 12-year-old boy. His life is spent gaming. This even stops his homework being done. His friend, Simon, always tries to get him off to go out. He won't.

It was 5pm in early August and James was gaming. Simon came in and dragged James off. They walked together into the woodland next to James' house. They found a clearing they hadn't seen before. They wandered in and as they reached the centre, they heard gunshots and screams. James got closer and closer. He recognised the people from his games. What had happened? He'd ruined everything!

ALEX GOUGH

Nunnery Wood High School, Worcester

THE LIGHT IN THE WINDOW

A wood. At dusk. Two young lumberjacks, Henry and Phil, were walking home. They noticed a bright, flickering light in the window of the ancient mansion, they were intrigued and wondered where the light was coming from. It was Henry who suggested they investigate, Phil refused but Henry advanced courageously, alone.

The dust inside choked him, the pictures of former inhabitants seemed to stare down at him. Mice scuttled as he found the wooden staircase and silently tiptoed towards the door. As he pressed his hand on the handle, he felt a cold, clammy hand on his neck...

THOMAS DARBY

Nunnery Wood High School, Worcester

CHILD IN WHITE

Darkness swept through the dense forest around Seth, he had nowhere to go and nowhere to hide. He was anxious. The night; desolate and silent, was closing in on him. Glaring around, Seth spotted an ancient, abandoned building, his only hope. Upon entry, a shiver ran down his spine. Something wasn't right. Sneaking down a deserted corridor, a sudden spark of light appeared. A short figure, its white dress was filthy and torn, its crying eyes dripping red. Hair, ink-black, dragged behind it. Seth was petrified. Turning quickly to run, 'it' clutched his leg. Who was it?

LUCY EVANS (12)
Nunnery Wood High School, Worcester

THE PLAYGROUND

Why am I coming this way? The playground's here, I usually avoid it. I'm sure my mind is playing tricks on me. Laughter is ringing in my ears, screams, shouts, echoes all around me. However, there's no one here. The swings and roundabouts are moving as if there are people here. The noises stop. Nothing's moving. It must be my imagination. I carry on, but my name is being shouted, almost cried, 'Sam... ! Sam... ! Sam... !' I'm rooted to the spot. A hand grips my shoulder. I should have believed my friends. I'll be lucky if I make it out alive...

OLIVIA NEATH
Nunnery Wood High School, Worcester

DEATH BY WAX

Sally crept along the corridor of the former waxworks, only the light from her torch illuminating the dummies that were enveloped in dust. Suddenly, a face appeared, stricken with fear, she ran into another room. As she entered, her attention was drawn to the large pot of boiling wax. Unnervingly, a deep, heavy breathing came from behind her. A bony hand reached out and grabbed her shoulder. Sally twisted around, her gaze met by a hooded figure dressed in black. Before she could scream, she was plunged into the boiling wax, immersing her whole body, encasing her for eternity.

JAMES THATCHER (12)
Nunnery Wood High School, Worcester

THE NIGHT

The fog flooded in. It sent shivers around the house. The thick mist flew around the haunted house. Ben entered cautiously. He glimpsed around.
He exclaimed, 'Anyone in?' He glimpsed again. Still nothing to be seen. Shuffling around, he opened a door. It creaked open. *What could be around the corner?* he wondered. The door slammed shut behind him. Dust glided off the window sills. The ancient clock started ticking again. The light was flickering on and off; it wouldn't stop! Bats flew around him, surrounding him, fighting him! What could Ben do?

OSCAR BIRD (12)
Nunnery Wood High School, Worcester

THE BOY IN THE WOODS

Gerald and his family loved camping. As their car clanked through the woods, Petal stared at the trees, imagining they were alive.

On arrival, Gerald set up with George. George saw a ghostly man, but while he was watching him he vanished.

As the family slept, they heard screaming. Gerald rushed to the other tent, pausing only at a red handprint. Entering, he saw Petal covered in blood. Grabbing George, he ran for the car. As he hurtled along the track, behind him the ghostly figure was smiling as the car crashed into a tree, becoming a ball of fire.

ALEX SKUTT (12)
Nunnery Wood High School, Worcester

CREEPERS' CHILLS

One moonlit night Dave was having a party whilst Sarah and Tom were out. As Sarah returned, she caught Dave partying. Then an earthquake struck. All three were knocked out.

As they awoke, everything was deserted except for zombies. As the zombies attacked them, they escaped by slaughtering them. They didn't have a home and needed to survive.

When they escaped, they got ambushed by zombies whilst resting in a cave. Thomas got dragged away and his brains were eaten. Dave and Sarah survived. A name travelled through the wind, 'Morro'.

MATTHEW PALMER (12)
Nunnery Wood High School, Worcester

WOLF HOUSE

AJ was an architect, he was examining a dilapidated mansion that was said to be cursed. As AJ entered the gloomy mansion, a shiver ran down his spine because of the ghostly look of the house. There were paintings on the crumbled walls of the previous owner's house. The labyrinth was full of endless whispering that suddenly stopped now and again.

Later on that night, AJ crept around a corner and saw a hairless wolf with silver eyes that shimmered in the moonlight and that were flashing through the ripped curtains. What happened after that? Nobody knows...

JOE EVANS (12)
Nunnery Wood High School, Worcester

FEAR IS NOTHING!

'Lucy, Lucy!' It came from the isolated dentist's surgery. Owls hooted around me. Cautiously, I walked up the drive. Lightning struck. My face went pale. I knocked on the door. The door flung open. A hundred bats soared out. A shiver ran down my spine. The voices lured me to a random hallway. I stopped, petrified. I heard a scream from the door beside me. Carefully, I opened the imposing door. There was nothing there! *How strange,* I thought. I took a step in. *Bang!* The door slammed behind me. I jumped. A cold hand touched my shoulder...

AMY DALE
Nunnery Wood High School, Worcester

THE CHURCH THAT GOT DESTROYED...

Bob anxiously trudged along the church pathway at dawn. It was his first shift as the church site cleaner. The night was gradually getting desolate. It was silent. Cleaning up the horrid mess the builders left made him fatigued. While cleaning up the boulders, he suddenly heard a voice whisper, 'I'm coming.' He started to panic as a shiver ran down his spine. He heard it again but louder this time; he wasn't going to take any chances and was ready to run. That split-second he was setting off, he was halted. It was something disgusting... What was it?

IBRAHIM ALI MAHMOOD (12)

Nunnery Wood High School, Worcester

ASLEEP

'It's OK, it'll all be OK,' the man in the white coat whispers as I feel the liquid pump into my blood. My vision turns into a sea of black, everything's gone.

My eyes snap open. Around me is a city, tall buildings tower above me and I can hear hums of growling throughout the streets. I trudge around. The growling noise has got louder. Suddenly, a hand grabs my shoulder. I'm grabbed down. As I float into hospital, I see the man wearing a large, shining white coat, peacefully watching my death turn into my most plain, final reality.

HANNAH WARSON (11)

Nunnery Wood High School, Worcester

CORPSES

Crash! Waves violently smash into the hull of your ship. You climb out of the hammock and start to wander around. You hear the buzzing of flies and become curious about the gut-wrenching stench. Pinching your nose, you run onto the top deck gagging for fresh air. You expect the rest of the crew to greet you. To your horror, you see a pile of rotting corpses, your crew. Devastated, horrified, you desperately burst into the captain's cabin... The captain's half-eaten corpse is slumped in his chair. Now you're stuck in the Atlantic Ocean, alone...

ETHAN MCDONALD-SMITH

Nunnery Wood High School, Worcester

OUIJA

The board lay there, still and silent but as terrifying as ever. Six girls had decided to meet at midnight in the attic of an abandoned warehouse. Upon arrival, they opened the door with slight hesitation. They crept up the staircase and finally made it to the attic. They sat around the board, too nervous to move. Lydia, the bravest, placed the glass cup in the centre. The others followed. 'Are you there?' whispered Lydia. The glass screeched - Yes. Sarah, the youngest, ran to the door screaming but her path was blocked by an ancient and rusty china doll...

EMILY MAIDEN (14)

Nunnery Wood High School, Worcester

THE EMPTY TOMBS

He was furious as he ran. He couldn't believe he'd just run away from home like that. Gerald didn't know where he was going, anywhere away from his angry parents at home. He was regretting the argument. Suddenly, it was getting dark and he came across a church graveyard. The moonlight reflected eerily on the fresh gravestone. He decided to camp out by a tree. When the morning dawned, Gerald could tell something was different. The graveyard somehow looked emptier. Then he saw it... all the graves were empty! There was suddenly a bone-chilling scream...

LLOYD RAWLES
Nunnery Wood High School, Worcester

THE WOODS

I'm waiting for my sister to come out of the eerie, foggy, murky woods. She had been in there for five minutes but we were together. I see her now, her silhouette heading towards me, I shout her name, 'Anna!' Nothing, I try again, 'Anna, is that you?' Her shadowy figure disappears into a house, a frightening, abandoned timber house. I run to grab her but she's already inside. I hear screams. I panic and enter the house. Nothing's there, I search. A corpse, not Anna's. I see paw prints leading upstairs so I go to investigate...

DESTINY VIOLET HARBORNE (11)
Nunnery Wood High School, Worcester

I SEE A GHOST

It was a dark night, the rain was beating on the windows, the moon beamed, lighting the room. The floorboards squeaked. I knew I wasn't alone. Something flew past me. Slowly, I looked around the silent room, I saw it! A glowing creature, floating. Chains hung from its body. Its eyes fixed on me. It flew across the room, stealing whatever it wanted. I couldn't stop it. Silently, the ghost hovered over to me. It brought out a knife, ready to stab me...

Beep! Beep! 'Wake up Peter, you will be late for school!' shouted my parents.

IMOGEN FORD (12)
Nunnery Wood High School, Worcester

EXPECT THE UNEXPECTED

Once, there was an old Tudor house that stood alone on a hill. In the house lived a horrible childminder. Nobody knew that though. *Knock!* A lady with three children banged on the door. The childminder opened the door. As the mother left, the lady took the children down to her basement. The basement had flickering lights and a sign on the dirty wall saying: 'RIP'. There were beds with chains.

'Ouch!' said the girl when she tried to get up. She screamed and woke up the others up and they all screamed, 'Help me, please!'

CHLOE WELCH (11)
Nunnery Wood High School, Worcester

Hospital's Child

Imagine me, a famous billionaire, sleeping rough. I ramble along the dusty path. Reaching into my pocket, I find my phone. I turn it on. A black screen stares back. No charge!
The bricks crippled like a pensioner, the door a protecting rock. Inside I creep to the nightmare room I know well. I hear a blood-curdling cry, I sprint out to the corridor. A misty creature, cradling a baby, stands crying a waterfall. She seems familiar - my deceased mother - younger; my brother in her arms!
Is it my mother or my imagination? My brother or my mind?

Freya Elizabeth Lawrence (12)
Nunnery Wood High School, Worcester

The Abandoned House

I was walking with my friend, Tom. Suddenly, I heard a creak at the abandoned house. It was the door. Tom and I ran to the abandoned house. The door creaked again. Tom stepped inside.
'No!' I shouted.
'Why?' whispered Tom.
'Because someone could live there!'
'So what?' laughed Tom.
'Fine, we will go inside,' I shouted. 'Tom, where are you?'
'Boo!' shouted Tom.
'Don't scare me like that!' I laughed. 'Tom, where are you? Tom?'

Millie Louise Yeomans (11)
Nunnery Wood High School, Worcester

I've Caught You Red-Handed

There was a haunted, dilapidated school surrounded by vines that crawled up towards the windows. As we walked into school, the floorboards creaked. My hands were sweating. Suddenly, there was an ear-piercing scream that echoed into the distance. A man appeared with a black rusty gun. As the man stepped closer, a shiver ran down my spine. My friends screamed, I was too scared to say or do anything. My life was going to be over. I died that night. My parents were devastated. My friends never set foot in the ghostly, spooky, haunted school ever again.

Gemma Thomas (12)
Nunnery Wood High School, Worcester

Hotel Of Secrets

One evening, after school had finished, Michael and Scott were walking down the sidewalk in New York. To avoid crowds, they walked down an alley. At the end was an old hotel which looked abandoned. They entered through the side door. It was dark with no electricity and no lights.
'Here Scott, this way,' Michael said. They went down the hallway. It was dark and they could hear footsteps and eerie music playing. They peered through the door and couldn't believe what they were seeing.. A dance hall full of ghostly figures dancing around!

Charlie Mogg (11)
Nunnery Wood High School, Worcester

IS IT HERE?

'Mum, can I go to Jack's party, please?' I enquired.
'Yes,' she replied.
I started to walk to the party. I saw house number 13, that was what it said on the invitation. It said to walk in. 'Hello?' I shouted, slamming on the wooden door. There was no response. I was getting worried. I started to walk around. *Click!* I thought that was the heavy door locking. I went to check and it was. What was I going to do? I was trapped in a house with no food or water. Then I heard footsteps. 'Hello...?'

JACOB BROADHURST (12)
Nunnery Wood High School, Worcester

THE HUMAN HUNTER

Ducking under a snowy branch, I stumbled clumsily into a clearing, fumbling in my pocket I retrieve my gloves just as it started to snow. I heard a distant scream, thinking it was just kids playing but then gunshots emanated from where the screams came! Crossing the stream, I spotted footprints... bloody footprints! They seemed to be dragging something. I stopped dead - a cabin with lights on! I rushed towards it. Suddenly, an eerie feeling came over me as I pushed the door open. All over the wall of the cabin were hunting plaques, one with my name on.

RYAN MOORES (12)
Nunnery Wood High School, Worcester

HE'S COMING...

The girl stood, terror seeping through her blood. She clutched her teddy close as she looked around at the abandoned fairground, not a soul for miles around. That night was dark and gloomy, the air dank. Then, she heard it. The music, fairground music, playing slowly and quietly behind her. She turned around... and then she saw it. A dirty circus clown stood by the carousel, hands by his sides. The girl dropped her teddy, turned, and ran. The clown lumbered over to the teddy, picked it up, and grinned. He started to chuckle. This was going to be fun...

CHLOE EMBLEY

Nunnery Wood High School, Worcester

THE MAN IN THE MIRROR

He's always there, always had been. Every time I pass, he's there staring at me. Today, it's different. The man in the mirror stands closer. No longer just in the shadows. I spin quickly, no one's there. Back in the mirror, he still stands, staring. The window flies open; this time, not just in the mirror. 'Something is different', was my last thought before a piercing pain erupted through my back. I want to see the man in the mirror before I go. He has a gun. The pain goes. Then I know nothing. He's still in the mirror...

AMY JOY JOHNSTON

Nunnery Wood High School, Worcester

GRIFFIN

The bird hovered in the strong wind above the village. He stared and stared and waited for the right moment to swoop and demolish his prey. As the last cloud passed and the opening was clear, he was ready. He descended quickly, as fast as lightning, through the wind to reach the land. He kept airborne with four large wings and flew across the grassy landscape, making his way towards the village. He lowered his sharp claws. The helpless village saw the bloodthirsty bird approaching. With swipes from the claws and strikes from the beak, they were gone!

ELLIOT DOTTI (13)
Nunnery Wood High School, Worcester

WHO'S THERE?

Skylar was an adventurous, brave girl. Her favourite place to adventure in was the haunted graveyard. Her mother told her not to go in the abandoned house. She didn't listen.
One day, she went to the graveyard. She was bored so she decided to venture to the house. It was pitch-black. As she tiptoed in, she heard loud screams and laughter everywhere. She felt a chill run down her spine. She carried on. Skylar was drawn to a black door. She turned the handle and slowly whispered, 'Who's there?' She was never to be seen again.

LIBBY KERMEEN (13)
Nunnery Wood High School, Worcester

The Haunted House On Malvern Hills

You creep through the forest, you notice a high wall parallel to you. You decided to climb the wall. On the opposite side, you see a house. You've never seen this house before, yet it looks like it should belong there. You creep closer, a wall of fog appears behind the house. It quickly engulfs the house, obscuring your view. Suddenly, the fog vanishes. You crawl forward until you feel something, eyes burning into your back. You whip around and there she stands, mystical and terrifying, dressed all in black. The lady of the Malvern Hills. Ghost!

Robert Sands (14)

Nunnery Wood High School, Worcester

Jack-In-The-Box

Back and forth, back and forth, that's what the jack-in-the-box did, the one my wife gave me before she died. Then, a deafening screech filled the room. A blinding light shone out of the box, then darkness. *Clunk! Clink! Clunk! Clink!* The heavy footsteps of the unknown came towards me, my worst nightmare - a 7ft clown towering above me with an iron hammer, my son's own head impaled on top. A ray of sunlight shone on the devilish clown's face. My last glimpse of life. *Splat!* Clown year had just begun. 'Hee-Hee!'

James Bradshaw (12)

Nunnery Wood High School, Worcester

The Heartless Demon

Murder. I love murder, it feeds the demons inside me. Stopping them from killing my mind. It hurts. I need more murder. I need the pain to go away. To be free from myself. *Thud! Thud! Thud!* Yes, Gerald is coming back with my next victim. I smile to my next victim. I smile to myself and begin to chuckle. She's pretty and blonde. She's perfect. My demons love blondes. I prepare myself. Overcome with joy. I love it. Her heart is what I desire. The doll has been waiting. I've been waiting. Soon I'll be free from my demons.

Milly Cobley (13)

Nunnery Wood High School, Worcester

Lost

It was a lovely day and two friends decided to go for a walk. They came across an abandoned house. 'Cool!' shouted Jeff.
'But it's getting dark!' said Jack.
'So?'
'But we need to get home because we don't have any idea how to get out of this field,' worried Jack.
'Doesn't matter because we have our phones,' said Jeff.
'But I have no signal, Jeff!'
'Oh!' shouted Jeff.
By now it was pitch-black and very chilly...

Elliot White

Nunnery Wood High School, Worcester

Suicidal Wolf

Once upon a time there were three thirsty piggies, planning their haunting revenge on the wolf. They were impressively good at being ghosts. They went frantically into the air towards the innocent wolf, it was the sinister black Friday when the pigs decided to get their revenge. The three fearless pigs went into the bad wolf's dream. The dream was about the wolf getting hurt by his worst nightmare. The three pigs told him immediately, 'You must die!' The wolf, who was innocent, continuously walked to his death until he woke up...

Shoaib Mohammed (14)
Nunnery Wood High School, Worcester

Don't Play With Fire

My sister died last year, in a fire at her house. I needed to be with her, so I moved into where she once lived.
As I stood outside the house, I tried to smile, but I just couldn't. I struggled to the door, my suitcase trailing behind me. As I cautiously stepped inside, I remembered it was 10pm, so I flopped onto the silk covers and dozed off.
Suddenly, the sound of light footsteps flooded my ears, I went to investigate.
I reached the basement, it was silent, until... A figure of flames appeared. It was my dead sister.

Imogen Pinder-Hampton (12)
Nunnery Wood High School, Worcester

The Phantom Lake

It all began in the manor. I was in bed that first, monstrous night, when shrieks pierced my ears. I flicked on the torch in my sweaty, tingling palms and crept outside; there was nothing. Nothing but the ghostly galleon in the sky. Anxious, cautious, vigilant, I decided to slip towards the lake, that was my biggest mistake. I gazed into the murky, icy depths, I saw nothing; not even my own reflection. An anonymous hand shoved me in, my hands flailed upwards, there wasn't even a splash. I glimpsed a sneering face, red hair, just like mine...

Agnas Linas (12)
Nunnery Wood High School, Worcester

Mirrored

The fog was creeping in. Walking, running, reaching out for me. How could I do that to myself? I regretted everything I said to my parents now. Rain was pounding. It ripped through the ragged fog as if it was nothing. Something that I couldn't do myself. Up ahead, was a vast mansion. Out of desperation, I pushed onto the rusted handle until it gave way. I huddled inside. Empty. The only thing present was a mirror. I peered at my reflection. The figure shifted, breathing. In condensation it wrote: 'Come play with us, Charlotte!'

Zoe Ma
Nunnery Wood High School, Worcester

MINE 13

I'm ready Mine 13... I enter the elevator that descends into the abyss. The elevator door opens and draws me into the darkness. *Crumble!* The mine has blocked both ends, I'm trapped within! I hear a sound rolling towards me. I turn around, there's a skull; a past miner. There are bite marks over it. I hear footsteps behind the wall of earth. They get louder, closer every time I blink. Suddenly, in front of me; red eyes, black demonic body. I stand still in fear. Nowhere to run. Another victim of the terror of Mine 13...

PRITHVI SATHYAMOORTHY VEERAN (12)
Nunnery Wood High School, Worcester

NIGHTMARE HOUSE

It was a dark and stormy night, a strange house appeared in the mist. The lightning was somehow attracted to the tower, it was magnetic. The windows were shattered. The whole house was destroyed. I walked through the destroyed gate, I looked back and the gate slowly rebuilt. I decided to touch it. 'Argh!' My hand felt like it was touching a block of ice at -500 degrees Celsius! I managed to survive without my hand! I quickly ran into the house, hoping someone could help me. I saw a ghost, then the roof collapsed on me. 'Nooooo!'

BRANDON COLIN NORMAN HARRISON (12)
Nunnery Wood High School, Worcester

THE MOVING TATTOO

'... and done!' Her tattoo was finally finished. But something felt strange about it. A sense of eeriness.

Later that night, she went to bed and realised that the dragon tattoo was the worst decision she had ever made.

The next morning she woke up to see that her tattoo had gone, and had its claws at her throat! Was this the end for her? Or could she save herself? She couldn't. She died ten minutes later from claws at her throat. As for the dragon, he flew away to live on a cold, snowy mountain for all eternity.

ELEANOR HOLLAND

Nunnery Wood High School, Worcester

DAD

Dad passed away ten years ago today. It's been so hard without him. Anyway, I was in the woods with Sarah and Ella. It wasn't my favourite place. *'Arrrgghhh!'* Ella vanished into thin air. My heart thumped 100 times faster as a chill ran down my spine. Not knowing what to do or where to go, we froze. A suspicious shadow appeared through the hand-like trees. It was clear it was here for only one reason, to kill us! Sarah turned around and ran as fast as her legs could carry her. He came closer, then I knew... it was Dad!

MILLIE ALFORD (12)

Nunnery Wood High School, Worcester

ZOMBIE DAD

Fog was rolling in, crows chirped and wolves howled. All of a sudden, *boom!* One of the graves shot up into the night sky. I was in a graveyard. A zombie climbed out of an open grave. 'Dad!' I shouted. My dad was a zombie. He had been transformed during the zombie apocalypse! All of a sudden, my zombie dad attacked me. Using only my bottle of water, I floored him and put the antidote down his throat. He survived, wobbled around and started coughing. About five seconds later, he turned into a human again. 'Jim!' he said.

ROBERT HOLMES (12)
Nunnery Wood High School, Worcester

THE DISAPPEARING GIRL

Heather and Daniel travelled home in the night, lost and confused. After an hour, they came to a part of the forest where the fog seemed to make the place seem haunted. There stood a girl, pale as snow, in a torn, white dress. The couple came to a stop, wondering what this little girl was doing out late.
'Come in, we can give you a lift home,' replied Heather.
They set off with the address. Sometime later, they came to the house where she lived; when Daniel looked back, he found she had disappeared! Where had she gone?

JUBIYA BIJU (12)
Nunnery Wood High School, Worcester

THE FINAL TRICK OR TREAT

Halloween; the most immoral time of year. Enjoyed by many due to its promise of amusement and treats, abhorred by me for its yearly sacrifice. His steps, those lethal and unfortunate motions he made, edged him towards the house, her house. My heartbeat faster than a race car on a track, I knew his sickening fate, his final fate. She would be there, sharpening her claws, perfecting her grip, grinding her teeth, ready to strike! I'm the cat, I follow them, watch them, wait for them to knock the door and make their final trick or treat...

ASARLA DIB

Nunnery Wood High School, Worcester

THE EERIE HOUSE

I walked into the forest. No one was there. I was alone. In the distance stood an empty haunted house. I walked closer, I saw something in the window moving about. It stopped. I quickly hid behind a tree. I slowly looked back, it was gone. My heart was beating faster than ever. Suddenly, rain started pouring down, so I had to go inside. As I opened the old, creepy door, the floorboards creaked. I slowly turned my neck. A big, white and yellow skull was staring at me from a shelf then, suddenly, my heart stopped beating. I'd died!

NED DERI (12)

Nunnery Wood High School, Worcester

ARE YOU OK DEAR?

Milly sat there, watching the world go by. Fog rolled over the dark, desolate park, a light wind touched her cheeks. From the corner of her eye, she watched as the swings slowly rocked. Suddenly, a young, pale girl appeared in a crimson stained gown, looking blankly towards Milly. Reaching out her hand, Milly made her way over. In a split second, the ghostly child had vanished, the park was empty again. Milly's head spun, heart thumping fast like the beat of a drum. A cold, frail hand touched her shoulder, 'Are you OK, dear?'

ERIN CLAIRE LAWRENCE-BURY (14)
Nunnery Wood High School, Worcester

INTO THE DARKNESS

I have to admit, I'm lost in the woods. I can feel the hairs on the back of my neck beginning to stand up. I begin to run. There is black ice everywhere. Someone runs into me. It is a boy. He grabs my hand. 'Come on, this way!' Weirdly, I can't help trusting him. 'I think we're OK. I'm Peter, what's your name?' Before I can answer, the monster appears, except this time he's accompanied by a man. Suddenly, he throws a knife. Peter jumps in front of me. I can feel cold metal cutting into my flesh...

RUBIA AMIN
Nunnery Wood High School, Worcester

The Scream!

I was walking home from work as usual, when suddenly I heard a young girl screaming. I rushed to the house where the sound came from. It was an old big house that nobody lived in. I looked at the window and saw a black figure. I walked slowly towards the door, I opened it really carefully. I stepped in and said, 'Hello is there anybody here?' Then, suddenly, someone whispered, 'Get out, or else you will...' I didn't listen, I stepped forwards. Then, suddenly, someone ran quickly into me. I looked at him, then...

Aniesa Baceva (13)
Nunnery Wood High School, Worcester

The Beast Within

There it was. Number 13. The oldest and creepiest house in the city. There were strange tales about this place, tales of evil, misshapen creatures in the shadows, tales of gruesome deaths. Despite all this, I was determined to explore. I walked up to the ancient, gnarled piece of wood that served as a front door. I gripped the handle and swung it open. As I stepped inside, a gust of wind blew the door shut. Suddenly, I heard a deep, throaty growl. I saw a pair of menacing, scarlet eyes. A monstrous abomination stepped into the light...

Reuben Ironside
Nunnery Wood High School, Worcester

THE UNKNOWN

Mia and Mike were having a nice stroll through the amazing, wonderful, colourful woods. The breeze blew through the oddly-shaped trees. They suddenly saw, out of the corner of their eyes, a spiral-shaped road made from wood chippings, leading to a place they'd never seen before. They took a risk of life or death and followed the wood road. After the walk on the wood path, they came to the end. Stood in front of their faces was an abandoned, mysterious house. Out of nowhere, something grabbed Mia's arms and snatched her away...

VICTORIA JANE TAYLOR (12)
Nunnery Wood High School, Worcester

HAUNTED GRAVEYARD

I had a glance at the forbidden forest. Nobody had been in there for 4,000 years. I felt a rush of bravery as I slowly paced my way towards the forest. I entered the line of the stones circulating the entire perimeter of the forest. I heard a whisper, 'Florence.' I ran towards the light that followed the ghostly, glowing stag. I tripped. As my eyes slowly rose, a quick gasp flew out of my mouth like a jet plane. I was in a graveyard. *Crack!* I turned. The gravestone had cracked! Closer, closer, closer. *Scream!*

DEVON WILLS (12)
Nunnery Wood High School, Worcester

Subject 6 A5 Quarantined...

... was the first thing she saw when she opened her eyes. It seemed to be tattooed onto her flesh in black ink. There was no light apart from the glimmer produced from the hatch above her, but there was sound. A loud drone. She followed it down the corridor to an open door. When the lights flickered on, hanging from the ceiling was a beautiful young woman. Attached to her was a note saying: 'You'll never leave'. She realised there was only one way out of this place. She looked up to see a rope already waiting for her.

Isabelle Scarborough
Nunnery Wood High School, Worcester

The House

Lily, a beautiful girl, decided to go for a walk. Minutes later, she got lost! She slowly walked down a gloomy, silent road. Stood in front of her, a frightening house. Lily was curious and wanted to explore, so she did.
Lily gently opened the creaking, wooden door to find a dusty hallway. She took her first steps into the house... *Bang!* It came from upstairs, Lily cautiously looked around. She looked left and right, door number 13 stared at her. Lily took her chances and wandered into the room... 'Help me!'

Bobbie-Jo Stedman (11)
Nunnery Wood High School, Worcester

Intruder

Screaming! I woke up with a sudden movement. I heard knocking on the door. I ignored the call and stood up ready in position. I slowly walked towards the door, ready for whatever was coming. 'Who's there?' I quickly opened the creaky door. Nobody there. 'Whoever it is, you'd better leave now!' I walked back to my room. It didn't feel right. I shivered in fright. Walking to the kitchen, I heard the fridge open. I definitely knew something was wrong. I rushed for the phone, turned, 'You're dead!'

Jago Fortey (12)
Nunnery Wood High School, Worcester

Terror From Within

The earth began to shake as Will walked past the ancient ruins of the castle. A bright light shone from the window of one of the upper windows. Will approached the large oak door, sealed for ten centuries. Outside stood a large oak tree, blowing in the wind. Will took a breath before kicking down the door to the unnerving sight of the ruin. No walls. No matter how hard he tried, he couldn't find the source of the light. He felt something behind him, turned around and saw Niall and Dylan, the evil twins. Will was never seen again.

Jack Beaman
Nunnery Wood High School, Worcester

THE DEATH OF THE VAMPIRE KING

On one damp, soggy spring day, my school was going on a trip to a very weird forest to discover some of the abnormal wonders. When we arrived, it was really dark. We walked in the forest, it was petrifying. *Roar! Bang!* I wanted to observe what was going on, I couldn't see. I was lost! *Bang!* 'Ow!' I couldn't see anything! When I got my vision back, I was tied up to a wall in a terrifying cave with two very paranormal people. One of them had wings on his back and was muttering, 'Roar! Beast!'

EMMANUEL ADESOLA (12)

Nunnery Wood High School, Worcester

DESERTED?

I landed on what I thought was a deserted planet. It was clearly devastated by nuclear war... As I started to search buildings, I started to hear voices! *Boom!* A bomb exploded. I remember wondering, *Who set it off? Why did they set it off and am I really alone on this planet?* As the mushroom was visible in the distance, I ran straight to my ship - it wasn't there. The sand started to shift, I saw a head in a mask poke out and start levitating with no body. I ran as fast as I could but... 'No!'

BENJAMIN ALLEN

Nunnery Wood High School, Worcester

A MIDNIGHT NIGHTMARE

The ancient window slammed open. A hammering echo filled the room. Abby climbed out of bed to shut it when she heard a distant, faint scream that triggered her thoughts. Abby felt so terrified and anxious that she crept on her tiptoes to her parent's room. The room was empty and it was trashed. She heard something, steps, footsteps, someone was there. Abby panicked, she was horrified. She hid. The wardrobe was dark, damp and musty, it was better than nothing. Someone or something opened the door an inch, it was the end of her.

JAMES PALSER (12)
Nunnery Wood High School, Worcester

THE DERELICT CIRCUS

Lucy saw an old leaflet on the ground. The storm blew it into her face, making her unable to breathe for a heart-stopping moment before she tore it away. The leaflet was red with Gothic print. Her eyes were fixed to the writing, which advertised a circus to be held at the end of the lane. A deafening flash of lightning revealed the outline of the derelict Big Top. She entered to the sound of the circus theme ending with static and an evil cackle. The last thing she saw was the hideously distorted image of the clown's face...

EMER HANCOCK
Nunnery Wood High School, Worcester

WHERE IS THIS?

I'm walking down the street. Charlie was meant to meet me 15 minutes ago. The streetlight flickered. I hate it when that happens. I call Charlie. Great, no reception. I make my way to the phone box. The wire is cut. Where the hell am I? It's getting dark and cold. I walk to the closest shop. The lights are out. What's this place? I call out for Charlie. The fog rolls in. There's a loud scream. I run. Far. I stop to breathe. An icy hand grips me. I turn around. It's Charlie but something is wrong, very wrong.

ISSY SAWYER (14)
Nunnery Wood High School, Worcester

BOBBY WITH A CHAINSAW

Bobby had just died. 'He was a very good man who didn't deserve to die,' said his wife. Suddenly, a noise came from his grave. They dug it up. Blood was all over the place. They pulled off the lid and the body was gone!
The next day, his wife went outside, the swing was swinging, a doll sang ring-a-ring o 'roses. She went over and said, 'Hello.' The doll didn't speak. It pulled out a chainsaw and killed everyone. Suddenly, within the space of a week, the human race was near extinction.

ELIOT TURNER (13)
Nunnery Wood High School, Worcester

Mystery Night

I was walking home but the fog drowned me, hiding everything so I couldn't see. I found an ancient, abandoned shack that I could sit in to ring Lizzie. My lips were trembling, I had a spine-chilling feeling. Lizzie rang back. 'Ruby, are you OK?' My battery died and I dropped to the floor in despair. Lizzie found where I was but not what I was after. All she saw was my bag and phone. Something was written in blood: 'I've found you'. I saw Lizzie break down as she thought she had found me. Bye, my friend.

Molly Ford (13)
Nunnery Wood High School, Worcester

Running In The Woods

Her footprints left trails in the damp mud of the woods. A faint beating of her heart echoed throughout the silent, misty night. It wasn't long before her breathing caught. The trees were hovering above the ground. Her life was in critical danger as she heard the wolves howl from the rocky cliff. Oxygen was being grasped from her lungs as her chocolate-brown hair blew fiercely against the strong wind. Footsteps got louder and she got lower. The ground pulled her in discreetly and soon she was enveloped in the city of fire.

Cortni Lamb (12)
Nunnery Wood High School, Worcester

Jason, Where Are You?

I arrived at the churchyard where I always met my friend. He wasn't there yet so I decided to wander. I opened the church door, someone told me it was haunted but that was probably just a rumour, I walked in and the door slammed shut behind me. I felt a cold shiver run through me, I went to run out the door; I tried to open it, it was locked. 'Jason, can you hear me? Are you there?' 'Molly!' he shouted back.

'Help me!' I yelled. 'Jason?' I never heard him talk back again.

Molly Daniels (12)
Nunnery Wood High School, Worcester

I Went Down!

Bang! Another man down. I knew it was going to be a hard time. It smelt like home, bread cooking. 'I miss you,' I groaned to myself. I was sitting in trench 31, damp and cold. I could smell the bread but I could also smell the dirty sewers. 'Are you there? What are you doing here?' She was gone again. 'Where did you go, beautiful wife?' All I could see was her floating head. I felt a tap on my shoulder. Slowly, I turned and my ear popped. I couldn't hear. *Bang!* Another man down...

Kai Phillip James Steer (13)
Nunnery Wood High School, Worcester

THE CURSE

Sophie was a girl who lived with her two sisters, brother, mother and father. One night, she was left alone in the house - Sophie was unaware that a shadow was within the walls. It was only a matter of time before it grabbed her by the neck. It muttered the words, 'You are deep in the burrows of my curse.' Thunder clapped hurriedly. In a flash of light, the figure was gone. A candle flickered in the distance but no shadow was to be seen. More importantly, Sophie was now part of a 'curse' - what did that mean?

ISABEL HUNT (12)

Nunnery Wood High School, Worcester

DEATH IS BLACK

A couple of years ago, something magnificent happened with a boy called Jeuse. His mum and dad were going on holiday so he had to go to his nan's for a weekend. Not just any usual weekend, a freaky one! It turned out that the house was haunted. Suddenly, at once, everything went silent. In the dark he turned around to see a black figure coming at him. He tried to run but walls started breaking down. He was stuck, he didn't know what to do. A white figure came and said, 'Son.' It wasn't his dad... was it?

KELSEY WATERS (12)

Nunnery Wood High School, Worcester

GREY

My name is Ava. I see the world differently to everyone else. I see the world in black and white. Dangerous things are always pitch-black, safe or good things are always pure white. My parents, of course, are glowing white and everything they touch is left with a glittery shimmer. I, like most people, am a boring shade of grey. I am at Mother's funeral. Though she is dead, her face is still shimmering in the dim light. However, when I look up at my father, he is suddenly the darkest shade of black, even in the light...

JASMINE RICHARDSON (13)
Nunnery Wood High School, Worcester

JAYNE, THE MYSTERIOUS FRIEND

Two girls were on their way to see their new friend, Jayne. As they approached the house, she greeted them with a suspicious look. She took them down to her basement to get a game. Suddenly, the door slammed! They heard an evil laugh. The lights flickered and the basement was revealed. Jayne took off her disguise, she was a witch! The basement was gloomy with thick layers of dust and cobwebs. Her mum then appeared in the doorway, holding a large item. She approached them with an evil look. Then their young lives were over.

NICOLA DUTSON (11)
Nunnery Wood High School, Worcester

Paintings

I am alone, in the famous killer's house. I walk round for a while, willing not to bump into the thing. There are paintings here, but there is something wrong with them all. It's as if they're not complete. As I look closer, I see a ghostly white rim in the shape of a human. *Boom... Boom...* Something is here. It knows I'm here. It's coming for me. As I turn, I see a man with no face. I'm being sucked in, into a painting! I can't move. I see flames... He's burning me alive! Help me!

Amy Adnett
Nunnery Wood High School, Worcester

The Abandoned Factory

Every day I would nervously walk past an abandoned factory. The old, rusty gate would creak in the wind. I always thought someone was watching me from inside the factory. When I looked back, no one was there.
Friday; it was finally time to go in. As I pushed the gate, my hands were dyed orange, it smelt of old metal. As I walked to the door, my heart was pounding out my chest. On the window someone had written: 'Go Away!' I was shaking, I knew as soon as I opened the door it would be my last breath.

Rebekah Dolphin (12)
Nunnery Wood High School, Worcester

EYES

You were there, so vulnerable and unsuspecting. Shivering by yourself, I bet you never thought I was stood behind you, waiting for you to turn around. You were having so much fun with all your friends until they left you on that cold, dark, cloudy night, all alone.

You felt a sudden gust of wind that launched you back and you fell into my grasp. Screaming piercingly for you life, you tried to wriggle out of my arms, It didn't work; all you did was turn to face me and I glared at you with my fiery red eyes...

MILLIE MCCORMICK
Nunnery Wood High School, Worcester

CLOSER THAN EVER BEFORE

It's there, watching, listening, waiting. Wherever I am, it is. It's always there. At first I thought it was my brother, he was the one who moved it, the one who started my nightmares, but he died a year ago. I see it out of the corner of my eye, never directly in front of me, but always coming closer. To start, it would sit across the room, eyes piercing into my back, now at arm's length. The pale china skin and golden locks imprinted themselves into my head. It stares at me now, closer than ever before...

DAISY DIXON
Nunnery Wood High School, Worcester

THRILLER

It was cold that night, the night when the fog covered my face like a blanket. I was creeping around the dark alley, scared that something might happen. Suddenly, I heard a loud moan in the far distance. It sounded deep and eerie. Intrigued, I ran towards the sound, slightly terrified but excited at the same time. I poked my head around the corner of the brick wall. I spotted a very unstable man stumbling around the abandoned courtyard. He had blood dripping from his mouth, then I realised... he was a zombie. Run!

NICOLE RUFF (11)

Nunnery Wood High School, Worcester

FIRST STAGE OF MADNESS

He woke up feeling nauseous. His vision was blurred. All he could hear was pounding against the window. Muffled screams came from across the hallway. The light kept flickering, irritating his eyes. He could hear chains bashing against the door, followed by the moans of an old man. The man couldn't move his body. All he could see were cuts on his arms and blood smeared all over the walls. He was helpless. Was this a dream or was this reality? He couldn't tell. There was a high-pitched scream. It was all over...

MATT ASHWELL

Nunnery Wood High School, Worcester

DIE

Tom and Maggie were playing football when Tom kicked the ball into the bush. They both went to get it and they saw an old, abandoned, dilapidated house. They looked at each other like they wanted to explore it, so they did. When they opened the old, rusty door, it creaked. They saw a mysterious, tall shadow. Tom stepped on something. He realised it was a head. They both screamed. They tried to open the door but realised it was locked. They tried the windows but they were locked too. Maggie shouted, 'Tom! Tom!'

AYAAN SIDDIQUE (11)
Nunnery Wood High School, Worcester

THE GHOST IN THE PIZZA SHOP

Tom and I were playing football when the ball flew into the forest. 'Oops, must have kicked it too hard!' Tom laughed. So Tom went to go get it. Before he knew it, he was surrounded by misty fog. I went to go find him but soon ended up at an abandoned pizza restaurant. 'Tom?' I called. 'Tom? Tom?' I called again. After five minutes of wandering around, I found Tom's army-patterned cap in a pizza box. Doors were slamming shut, windows were smashed. The only thing to do was to run in fear...

KAI TRENNAN (12)
Nunnery Wood High School, Worcester

GOODNIGHT MUMMY

On a dreary day, two boys, twins, were playing at sword fighting with sticks. They heard a car horn so the two brothers ran inside and said, 'Mama!' They ran upstairs to go find her. They went into her bedroom and she was staring at herself in the mirror with the fan blowing her clothes. The two boys said, 'Mama, is that you?' She quickly turned to them and walked over.
One of the twins said, 'You're not our mum.'
Suddenly, she got angry and slapped the boy's face.

JADE LOUISE BELL (14)
Nunnery Wood High School, Worcester

THE CHASE IS ON

Daylight was gone, blackness covered the sky. Two teenagers ended up in an old, crooked, big mansion. They had no choice but to stay for the night. While they were sleeping, at midnight, they heard noises coming from the graveyard. It was the killer of the night. They got up and found the killer in front of them. They shouted, 'Help!' They ran for their lives. All they had to do was run. He'd come to kill and sprinted at them. He sliced their heads off and stabbed them in the heart. Their arms fell off.

SOLOMON SONY (12)
Nunnery Wood High School, Worcester

The Mist

The boy sat at the window, surrounded by the crumbling bricks that formed a desolate tower. His eyes fixed on the silvery mist seeping out of the treeline. It formed the shape of his dead father, his hair thin and delicate like a spider's web. He shivered with shock, was this just a trick of the mist? The sight of his father caused him to go into a trance. He needed to get to the mist before it spread into the dying grass. Moving towards his father, he fell out of the window to his death. The mist disappeared.

Rosie Hibbard (13)
Nunnery Wood High School, Worcester

The Blazing Eyes

Looking terrified, Jane stumbled past her back door, scanning it in the process. She felt the rain pouring down her face as she ran down her garden. She stopped to see a shadow pass over her. She looked up. A hooded figure crept closer and with every step, her heart came closer to leaping out of her chest. It stopped in front of her. She looked up to see its blazing, yellow eyes staring at her with a sense of fear. 'Jane, Jane!' screamed her mother. She turned around. Her mother had the same blazing eyes.

Hannah Portman (14)
Nunnery Wood High School, Worcester

WHERE ARE WE?

Waking up, Gizmo, Thomas and I were confused about where we were. We saw a man with a tag that said 'Jet'. He took us into a room. Suddenly, we found... a diary! We took down the picture while Jet was gone. Behind it there was so much blood. We read the diary. It was written by James. All it said was, 'Don't take down the painting'. It was too late! A zombie-like figure grabbed Gizmo. He screamed and Jet laughed. It turned out Jet took us here and made us lose our memories, just so he could...

LUKE BLUNDELL (12)
Nunnery Wood High School, Worcester

SPOOKERELLA

One sunny day a little girl was born. The girl had no mother so she lived with her dad. Then, one day, her dad married a woman who was evil. Soon, her dad died. She was with her stepmum who was very mean to Spookerella. One day the stepmum told Spookerella to go to a cottage in the fields for some bread. Actually, there was another reason, it was to kill Spookerella. The abandoned cottage was full of dangerous traps. Spookerella nearly got caught! Just then, a man came and saved her. No more stepmum!

SANA ABDUL (11)
Nunnery Wood High School, Worcester

THE LONELY DOLL

It was getting dark, I still couldn't find her. I'd been looking for her for more than an hour! I couldn't see anything familiar. I needed shelter. As soon as I thought that, I saw an old, abandoned house. It was so cold, I felt like an ice sculpture so I crept inside. The door locked behind me. I felt a bit anxious. There was a creepy doll staring at me so I edged away from it. It turned its head. I froze. It started to move and it spoke! 'Don't go away, I want to play!' It pounced...

CHRISTINE HENN

Nunnery Wood High School, Worcester

LEFT ALONE

There was an old house at the end of the deadly street. Nobody knew anything about the house, except for one thing.
One day two twins decided that they were going to find out who lived there. As they opened the door, they found pure horror. As they carried on tiptoeing over the broken floorboards, the lights went off. All of a sudden, there was a blood-curdling scream. 'Argh!' It was a twin! His heart was racing, he was petrified about what happened. He tried running away, he was left alone.

WILLIAM BARRIE ROGERS (11)

Nunnery Wood High School, Worcester

CHINA DOLL

One stormy night, I heard a creak from the door of the abandoned house. The lightning shot across the top of the roof, a voice came from inside. I went inside to find a doll sat on a rocking horse, humming. I walked past the doll to find her eyes following me. I got to the window, looking outside. As I turned back, the doll had gone. Frantically looking... no sign of the doll. I ran for the door. Upon seeing my reflection, I touched my face. My face had become the china doll's face. How did this happen?

LILI MAI FLORENCE WORKER-MOORE (12)
Nunnery Wood High School, Worcester

THE VILLAGE OF DEATH

One summer's evening, four best friends set off for what they thought was going to be a great camping trip. How wrong they were. On the second night of the trip, there was a big storm. In the morning, Emma was gone. It was as if she had been swept away by the harsh, violent winds. She was gone. The three others decided to pack up and look around. They came across an old, abandoned village. There they found Emma with a scar on her face and a mysterious boy, Dan. As they left, Dan collapsed. He was dead.

MOLLY WHITE
Nunnery Wood High School, Worcester

THE KNOCK

It was 12.17am. I was asleep. I woke up to the sound of knocking. I crept downstairs to prevent waking anyone else up. I opened the door to a cold breeze but no one was there. 'Hello?' I called out. I didn't get a response. The door slammed shut by itself which caused me to scream. I ran upstairs to wake my dad up, but I tripped. I felt a cold breeze again. A cold hand touched my shoulder. I turned around to see who had touched me... no one was there. Suddenly, I heard a high-pitched scream.

CHLOE MORGAN WOODING (13)

Nunnery Wood High School, Worcester

HELLO MADDIE

I saw the house, I knew it wasn't a good idea. Its rotting porch nearly broke under my feet. As I walked through the doorway, a large, cold hand grabbed me from behind. I screamed, nobody came. The huge person dragged me up the steep stairs and sat me on a chair in the dust immersed attic. I saw his face for the first time, it was scarred and grimacing! Suddenly, with a shock, I woke up - it was a dream! Then, I saw him there in the corner of my room, the man from my dream. 'Hello Maddie.'

LYDIA HOWELL (11)

Nunnery Wood High School, Worcester

THE HORRIFIC HOLIDAY

It had been a terrible drive, we were finally there. On holiday! The weather was shocking, it was like we were in a horror movie! As we pulled up, lightning struck. The house looked gloomy. The sky was dark and the air smelt like death. I stepped through the door, I was blown away by how draughty it was, I was freezing. I was in the kitchen, I could feel eyes staring at me! The door creaked open. My heart must have jumped out of my chest, I was that frightened. I just wanted to leave. It was silent...

MOLLIE MONTGOMERY (12)

Nunnery Wood High School, Worcester

WEEPING WILLOWS

I knew they were coming, all along I should've know, tonight was the night they struck!
It was a normal day until I got home, I saw a mixture of oak and birchwood shavings. The main thing was that the door was hanging open, a chipped wood block was left in its place. It said, 'Say your goodbyes!' It felt like a bolt of lightning had broken through my heart, my parents were gone! I turned around for a closer inspection, I saw a withered corpse staring right into my beady eyes...

HANNAH MADDISON (11)

Nunnery Wood High School, Worcester

CAVE OF DOOM

Boom! I heard an explosion. I'd crashed my car into a forest. I slowly walked into the forest like a slug, looking for help. I didn't know how long it had been, there was no one in sight. I spotted a cave, I didn't dare enter. Unfortunately, it rained. I had to shove myself inside, my heart raced as an echo cried for help. There was a broken bottle on the floor. I saw a man... a fog man! I got chased. Running for my life, I was pushed over and dragged into a pit of dead bodies.

ANGAD SANGHA
Nunnery Wood High School, Worcester

THE GIRL

The bright, gleaming daylight was fading away. The midnight sun was dawning. It was dark, desolate; I was scared. I was wandering along the never-ending beach when I noticed a pale girl with long, dark hair standing in the distance. Curious, I walked over to ask for help, not realising I was asking Death. As soon as I said the first word, she revealed her monstrous face with fiery eyes and blades for teeth. I sprinted as fast as I could for as far as I could see. She was faster; I was going to die.

GRACE MORRIS (12)
Nunnery Wood High School, Worcester

THE FOREST

The car broke down and no one was around. The deadly silence was getting to him. How could he get home? There wasn't a garage for a couple of miles and he was starting to see things in the bushes. There were noises everywhere, it was getting cold and his phone had no signal. He went down the road to an abandoned asylum. The doors were open, the sign said: *Mental Asylum.* He picked up a document with a missing person on it. He heard a chainsaw and a man ran at him with it. He woke up...

CONOR WALTER WILLAM HOPE (13)

Nunnery Wood High School, Worcester

THE SHOCKING SHED

I was walking home from school through the forest. The wind was blowing and the leaves were crunching under my feet. I couldn't find the end, it felt like a maze. It got dark and I was still in the maze. I found a building and I ran up to it. I realised it was only an old, rusty shed. I started walking away but I heard something say, 'Come back.' It grabbed my hand then pulled me in. I searched but no one was there. I tried to leave but couldn't! The door was locked. I was trapped.

NATALIA OKRASA (13)

Nunnery Wood High School, Worcester

THE SPOOKY FIGURE

One spooky night, my friends and I decided to explore an abandoned asylum. As we went in, we saw a spooky, creepy figure lunge at us. We ran through the cramped corridor then, as we went through a door, we got locked in. We tried everything to get out but whatever we did, it didn't work. Suddenly, we heard a noise coming from the door. It knew we were there. We panicked more, it finally came in and we saw its horrible, disgusting face. We screamed for our lives. We were never seen again!

JACK DAVID BROOKS (13)

Nunnery Wood High School, Worcester

NO MORE

We went on a camping trip. We went just outside the Forest of Dean but a storm flew over, darker than the depths of Hell. We took our camping gear into the forest. The trees fought to escape, there was crying. A girl was crying against a tree, repeating the same two words, 'No more!' I went over to comfort her but when I touched her, she screamed, with the voice of 1,000 souls. A demon climbed out of her mouth, bringing more and more up with it. We ran, but not fast enough. We were dead.

WILLIAM REA

Nunnery Wood High School, Worcester

ALICE AND HORROR LAND

It was a warm day. Alice was having a picnic when she saw something in the corner of her eye. She panicked! Then she realised it was a bunny, not just any old bunny, a human-eating bunny! 'Oh no!' she said. The bunny ate her!
After, the bunny hopped to the blood-collecting queen. She took the blood. They lived happily ever after. But that's not how it ends. Someone caught the bunny... the pink cat! He made a wish and disappeared. They were never to be seen ever again.

CHLOE SMITH (12)

Nunnery Wood High School, Worcester

THE ROCKING DOLL

Fog was closing in, it was Christmas Eve. Time to give my wishes to my father at the graveyard. I was alone and cold. I had ice in my veins. I was frozen as I arrived. Just the presence of the graveyard made me shiver. I was there now. The grave we laid all those years ago, already covered with flowers. I was just about to leave when I noticed a doll, just rocking from side to side in the wind. Its eyes were wide, staring at me and nothing else. Suddenly, a hand touched my shivering shoulder...

WILLIAM TOLLEY

Nunnery Wood High School, Worcester

The Ghost At The Crash

I yelled in pain as our car collided with a wall. My leg was stuck and oil was dripping onto my face. I coughed and spluttered as the oil dripped into my mouth. I saw a person running towards me to help. They took off their jumper and held it against the roof to stop the oil dripping down. Then they freed my leg before dragging me away from the car. I saw an orange glow coming from the front, then the car exploded into pieces. They laid me down on the road and left, disappearing into thin air!

Sam Godby (13)

Nunnery Wood High School, Worcester

Two Went, One Returned

Rae and I set up camp near an abandoned churchyard. Later that day, I went to collect some firewood. When I came back, she was gone! Suddenly, I heard a noise. It was a man's voice, calling me. 'Katie! Katie!' I ran into the church. It was hard for me not to scream. A man was behind me. He was covered in blood. I whispered, 'I hope that's not Rae's blood.' He stabbed me, so I ran as fast as I could.
I woke up in a hospital. Rae was never seen again.

Abigail Tarbuck (12)

Nunnery Wood High School, Worcester

THE MOANING MANOR

It was the day that we moved house, well, I say house but it was more of a manor. A dense fog was settling and there was a freezing chill in the air. As we approached the new residence, I could swear that I heard a long moaning sound that struck fear into my heart. As we entered, a large apparition beckoned us in, but, once again, I was probably hallucinating. However, in my room, horrible figures grabbed me from under the bed and dragged me into a dark room where they fed on my soul...

JASPER STRUTHERS
Nunnery Wood High School, Worcester

DEEP, DARK WOOD

I was walking back from training with some friends, we were just about to enter the deep, dark woods. There was a storm approaching. We ran into the woods, trying not to get wet when lightning and thunder appeared. In a flash, my friends were gone, I was all alone. I could see things but I wasn't quite sure if it was an illusion. Crazy sounds in my head led me to a lake, with a sign saying: 'Dead Man's Lake'. I leant in to have a look, then I saw it, it was too late...

SARAH SMITH (12)
Nunnery Wood High School, Worcester

THE MYSTERIOUS CROOKED HOUSE

Rachelle, Abi and Katie were all shopping in town. As they left the town centre, they noticed an old, crooked house all by itself. They stood there for a moment. Suddenly, a dangerous carpet and string came out from the horrid house and tied the three girls up, dragging them in. The carpet left them, so they took a look around. As they looked around, one of the girls screamed. An old man had grabbed her. They used their secret power on him and escaped. Then they burnt the house down.

RACHELLE DAVIES (12)
Nunnery Wood High School, Worcester

THE HOUSE OF GHOSTS

Once, there was an old, decaying house. The house was surrounded by vines and dead animals. Crows sat on the broken aerial. As I walked in, the floorboards creaked. I saw a bright light in the distance. I walked towards it. I stopped and the moment that I hesitated, I heard a screech. What was it? Was it Henry? Had I finally found him? No! It wasn't Henry. Something grabbed me!
That was the day I died and now I am back, haunting the living. Good luck, living people.

LIBERTY FINCH (12)
Nunnery Wood High School, Worcester

THE DOLL

Every night we can hear noises. We have been here for four days. When we got here there was a doll but since then we haven't seen it! It's very scary here, there is also a grand piano in our cabin. Tommy has a room downstairs like me, and every other night there will be one or two notes played. We mainly ignore it but now it's getting more frequent we are thinking of leaving this place...
That's it! We are leaving. Tommy is dead - the doll strangled him!

LUKE REID (13)

Nunnery Wood High School, Worcester

SARAH'S MAID

I walked the hallway of our new house. A woman in a rocking chair was brushing her doll's hair. I wondered if it was our new maid. As I got into bed, that same lady came in and said that she was my maid. She would watch me until I went to sleep.
When I got up, the rocking chair was still rocking as if she had only just got up. I asked my mother about my new maid. She replied, 'A maid? There hasn't been a maid walking these floors for over 100 years!'

SOPHIE NICOLE SMITH (13)

Nunnery Wood High School, Worcester

INTO THE WOODS

On a cold, stormy night, my family and I stayed the night in a creepy hotel. Bloodthirsty bats stood on a tree, waiting to attack. I made my way up the dark and twisted staircase. I glared at a creepy doll on top of the window sill. I saw a sign saying: 'Meet me in the woods at night for a sweet surprise!'
As I slept, I heard a scream from the woods. I quickly dashed to the woods.
Ever since that day I've been missing!

ALAN MANOHARAN (12)
Nunnery Wood High School, Worcester

GHOSTLY SCHOOL

Once, there was an old, decaying school. Vines wrapped around the walls. As I crept through the abandoned halls, I heard a deep voice say my name. I turned towards the door where the voice had come from, I cautiously grabbed the handle tightly. As sweat dripped down my forehead, I slowly opened the door, creaking the hinges. I peered inside, I saw a terrifying figure... A ghost slowly turned his pale face towards me and sliced me in two. That was the day I died!

CRISTA EDMUNDS (12)
Nunnery Wood High School, Worcester

HOME ALONE

I was at home. I woke up yawning and decided to go downstairs. Where was everyone? Suddenly, I heard a loud bang! I went to go find out what it was. My heart was racing. No one, just a pan on the kitchen floor. How did it get there? Another noise came from upstairs, made by someone or something. I tiptoed upstairs as fast as I could. I found a trail of breadcrumbs that I started following. I was getting suspicious and petrified at the same time. It led me to a window...

ISRA MAHBOOB

Nunnery Wood High School, Worcester

NARNIA AGAIN

I went into Narnia. The magical Narnia. Or that is what I thought. When I arrived, it was gorgeous, peaceful autumn. Then it happened. Across a tree branch was the war of two sides. I observed for ages, watching it progress. Then it was dark, I was captured, like an enemy to the animals in power. I didn't know what was happening. I was scared. I was shoved in a hut and this is the only thing I found to write on. Oh no! They are coming and I'm awaiting my death.

INGA JACKSON (14)

Nunnery Wood High School, Worcester

SPINE-CHILLER

It was spring break. My name is Declan and my friends are called Josh and Brandon. We went on a trip for spring break, I was driving a Subaru and my friends were at the back of the car. We went past what looked like an abandoned house. It gave me the chills. Brandon asked if we could go in, so I said, 'OK.' I stopped the car and got out with my friends. When we opened the door, it creaked. We went in, scared. Josh came up with a knife and killed Brandon and I!

DECLAN LUNN (12)
Nunnery Wood High School, Worcester

THE CLOWN'S CHURCH

It was Monday night. I was at church alone. I went outside and saw some kind of shadow. I got itchy because it frightened me when I saw it. There were footsteps along the path, I followed them. A tree, tall and crippled, I looked at it. I saw blood. I sprinted home and I tripped over a twig, I looked up. There was the shadow again. There was a dead body and bones on the body. I walked back to my house. Then I stopped - there was a jack-in-the-box with a bloody clown.

JOSHUA RANDLE (12)
Nunnery Wood High School, Worcester

THE LABYRINTH

We started at the start line. The gunshot fired and off we went. Our first challenge was to find our way through a difficult-looking maze. The maze was made of what looked like 60-year-old sandstone. When we arrived, we noticed that there was a tatty-looking, fragile house made of wood. I had a funny feeling about it since all of the other teams had gone another way to us. In the distance, I could barely make out the shadow of an old man. He pointed his gun at us...

JACK CLAYTON (13)
Nunnery Wood High School, Worcester

BITE

Bang! Four people woke up and found themselves in a room with a snake. The snake was surrounding them. Then they fell down a hole and got knocked out when they hit the ground.
They found themselves at an abandoned school. They smelt an horrific smell and noticed it was the snake. They all ran into a little area and all found swords. They had a stare-off with the snake. They won and ran towards each other just as a vehicle came around the corner...

KYLE ANHONY GOPPY (12)
Nunnery Wood High School, Worcester

THE SPOOKY TAXI

It was a spooky night in the huge city of London. My twin and I needed to get a taxi home to our family home. We saw a taxi careering around the corner, so we shouted and he came hurriedly towards us. Now that we could see the taxi properly, we noticed that the taxi was mouldy and muddy. We both looked at each other and got into the eerie taxi. The man had long, tangled hair and black teeth. My twin fled the taxi, but I was captured by the horrible man ...

CATHERINE NICOL (12)
Nunnery Wood High School, Worcester

LINE OF DUTY

Dave and Jeff are soldiers and they are looking for a boat called 'The Blue Plank' in the spooky rainforest. Suddenly, Dave got lost and Jeff was scared so he walked back, trying to find him. He couldn't find Dave. Dave had found the boat and tried to ring Jeff, but got no answer. So he left Jeff in the forest. He shouted, 'Bye, Jeff!'
Dave saw the gold in the boat and celebrated. Jeff was all by himself. Would he get home?

JAYDEN SCOTT (11)
Nunnery Wood High School, Worcester

UNTITLED

I felt really cold, my hairs stood up. I sensed a creepy ghost. I heard my dog roaring in pain in the basement. I started to wonder what was happening. I turned on all of the lights, they flickered so I yelled out loud. My dad was acting weird, so I went upstairs, then I got thrown into the air. I knew it was the ghost. I saw a shadow in the window so I walked up to the window, then I looked out of it. A hand appeared so I ran, then I fell...

HARVEY ORMSBY (12)

Nunnery Wood High School, Worcester

THE TAILS DOLL CURSE

Bill and David got back from the local game store. As soon as they got in, they put in their new game. After ten minutes of playing the game, the doorbell rang and David opened the door. A doll plastered in blood was on the doorstep. He took it in and washed it off, then went back up to play. He heard a noise and went back. Suddenly, Bill heard a shriek from downstairs. The place was covered in blood. He felt a cold, wool-like hand holding his...

RYAN SIMCOCK (12)

Nunnery Wood High School, Worcester

My Dad The Undercover Hero

My dad came home from a 14-hour shift at work. He came in and put four chocolates out for breakfast for his four children. They saw him and the chocolates and hugged him. They said, 'Dad, we love you!' He had a shower and a bite to eat, then rested. After an hour, the children went to bed. He went to the gym in the cellar. The children were woken by a man crying for mercy. They ran downstairs where the voices were coming from...

Zara Zeb (11)

Nunnery Wood High School, Worcester

A Whole New World

It was a nice day and we were all playing in the forest. Jeff, Bob, Michael and Billy were with me as well. We were all playing catch when, suddenly, the weather got windy and a bit dusty. After, I saw a little light in the sky. That was when I saw it grow bigger. It was a huge portal that sucked everything in and took it to a whole new world! I jumped in there. I knew there was no return from this. We tried anyway. We jumped. No escape...

Hano Zana Baban (11)

Nunnery Wood High School, Worcester

CUT SHORT

I'm afraid of everything. No one can be trusted, every glance or touch makes my heart race. I'm terrified of what will happen if they find me. They can't find me, they'll hurt me, chase me, they want to cut me open, torture me. I'm their play toy and they're the Rottweilers. I have a day on which I'm supposed to die, my time is running out. If this is the last thing I write, I wouldn't be surprised. Goodbye.

CHARLOTTE WARSON (14)
Nunnery Wood High School, Worcester

THE DARKEST NIGHT

One Monday in March, it was a dark night. I was walking home with my friends. All of a sudden, I heard someone scream. I turned around, all of my friends were gone so I ran. It was a dead end. There were two men going to grab me, I screamed and two people came out of their house, they shouted at me to get off their land. They shot them! They grabbed me and ran. I was locked in the car. I couldn't stop screaming. There was a bang...

SIAN WILLIAMS (13)
Nunnery Wood High School, Worcester

THE HOUSE!

It was the creepiest house in the neighbourhood. It had broken windows and boarded up doors.

One dark day I went to check out the house. As I walked in, the door shut behind me. It was dark and gloomy. A hand fell from the ceiling, it pointed upstairs to the bedroom. I looked in, I saw a doll sitting on a rocking chair, singing, 'Tiptoe, through the window.' I suddenly felt a hand on my shoulder...

OLIVER DAW (13)

Nunnery Wood High School, Worcester

DEATH ZONE

Clouds engulfed the entire area. The black rusty gate creaked open. As I stepped in, I could taste evil. Dark faces popped up through the window, I knew this was not a safe house. I could hear footsteps approaching behind me, getting louder and louder. My heart pounded with fear and my eyes darted everywhere. Something or someone tapped me on my shoulder. I tried escaping, there was no way out. I realised it was my worst nightmare.

AQEEL MAHMOOD (13)

Nunnery Wood High School, Worcester

THROUGH MY HELL

Frank, Matt's best friend, died and Matt was looking for him. He found an abandoned mineshaft. He looked all over; left, right and centre. He began to exit and heard a call for help. It sounded like Frank. He ran and found the corpse. It wasn't Frank, it was a mob of the walking dead! A toxic fog floated behind them. In the middle was zombie Frank! He said, 'This is my living hell.' He ran, toxic fog following...

BENJAMIN KEVIN BOREHAM (11)
Nunnery Wood High School, Worcester

WILL I RETURN?

Was I ever going to get out? Was the school haunted? Was it going to be the end? As I walked into the haunted school, all I could hear was the thud of my heartbeat, the autumn leaves swaying in the distance. I was scared, everyone knew it. As I stepped into the forbidden school, a shiver ran down my spine, it was pitch-black and there was nothing in my sight. I tripped, my heartbeat grew louder. It fell silent. I died that day!

LOUISE CATHRYN CHURCH (12)
Nunnery Wood High School, Worcester

THE DOLL

In 1980, there was a new doll called Robert. It all changed when he came into this world. He came alive and started to kill people until there was one person left... me, Chris. I had to hide, he was coming for me. 'Robert!' He found me. I had to find something to keep me alive like a weapon. There it was, a gun. I grabbed it quickly and turned around as fast as I could. I started to shoot him. He was dead... or was he?

OWEN PAGE (12)
Nunnery Wood High School, Worcester

THE HAUNTED HOUSE

Stumbling, I walked into the deep, dark forest, there stood a big black silhouette, staring at me! I was petrified. I tried to run away. As I ran, I passed a tall brick house. I walked back towards the tall brick house and I went through the black gates, they slammed shut behind me. Noisy little dogs came out towards me. I ran like lightning.
I woke up in the morning to find it was all a dream.

ALANAH LEVETT (12)
Nunnery Wood High School, Worcester

HOME ALONE

I woke up to the sound of footsteps creeping up my stairs, I was really scared. My TV was still on so I muted it so I could hear them clearly. I was home alone, I knew it wasn't my mum or dad, and I had no pets. I jumped out of my bed and I hid under the covers. I covered my mouth so no one could hear my breathing. I stayed down, I could see his face. He had no eyes or mouth. I was dragged from my bed.

CALLUM COFFIN
Nunnery Wood High School, Worcester

KNIVES AND VINES

Stumbling into the dark forest, I came across an old mansion encased in old vines, they crawled up to the dusty windows. As I was a curious person, I decided to enter the house. As soon as I took my first step, I felt a cold, bony hand grab my shoulder. Suddenly, I had goosebumps, my nerves were on edge. I knew that it was the end. I slowly turned my head to see a sharp knife, before I knew it, it was in my heart.

ELEANOR SARAH PERRY (12)
Nunnery Wood High School, Worcester

What Lurks Below

When we moved house, I saw a door, I forgot about it for a few weeks but in the middle of the night, I heard a noise coming from below the house. I went to see what it was. When I got down to the basement, there was a lot of old stuff there. Then, I heard a noise from the other side of the room. When I heard it, I saw a family of raccoons. I bent down to stroke them, they tore my face off! I died that day.

Theodore John Stanley-Palmer (12)

Nunnery Wood High School, Worcester

HELLO HELL

The glimmer of the moonlight blinded me. The sudden panic touched every vertebra in my spine, before sending a bomb to follow in its tracks. The light of the moonlight vanished and left me, a rejected soul, empty inside. A bitter crisp shadow stalked me, its bleak breath suffocating. I took my final gulp, and set off towards Heaven, didn't I? Flicking my eyes open gradually, the mirror to Heaven was cracked. Who or what was in front of me? There were murky bulbs of red, glaring through my body, ghostlike. Heaven? I thought; no, Hell was my new home!

ELLIE MAE DENT (12)

Paulet High School, Burton-On-Trent

GRAVEYARD MYSTERY

I had been abandoned, left alone. Trapped in a graveyard. 'Kyon!' I cried. But there was neither sound nor movement. *Creak!* The gate shut. 'Help me!' I screamed. No one was there. Suddenly, I heard a rustling in the bushes. 'Who's there?' No answer, but then I heard a werewolf. *Arrrooo!* I started sprinting as fast as I could. The werewolf was right behind me. As I almost got to the gate, I fell. Kyon jumped on top of the werewolf and was scratched across the throat. The werewolf left. 'Kyon, nooooo!'

THOMAS WARD (12)

Paulet High School, Burton-On-Trent

DRAGON BREATH

There was something in the bushes, it wasn't my imagination it was real. I followed it through the bushes. Through the gloomy, shadowed trees, and into an old abandoned factory. It was like something that would give children nightmares as they slept, watching them in their dreams. I turned and watched the rusty door slam shut behind me. I was scared. I closed my blood-red eyes, hoping that I was asleep; I wasn't. A shudder of fear ran through my veins, there was something behind me. Its breath on my neck. It was fiery like a dragon.

PAIGE WILEMAN (12)
Paulet High School, Burton-On-Trent

THE DAY WHEN MY FRIENDS WENT MISSING

It was two weeks ago when my best friends went missing, it still haunts me to this day. I'll explain, it was a normal day at school, whilst in class, we saw a figure in the old abandoned house. The house had been there for centuries, there was a story about the creepy place. There was a young girl, mother and father. Somebody said that the girl killed her mother and father and then killed herself. Suddenly, I saw a shadow again and told my friends, they didn't believe me so they dared me to enter.

NICOLE WILSON
Paulet High School, Burton-On-Trent

FEELS LIKE IT WAS YESTERDAY

The terrible moment happened when I went to visit my nan like I always did on a Tuesday night. I unlocked the door and walked in. I shouted, 'Nan are you here?' Then I saw my grandad who had been divorced from my nan for a couple of years. I was shocked, standing there. Then my grandad came towards me. 'Look at this knife, I killed your nan, now I'm going to kill you.' I barely escaped with my life, it still affects me to this day. Now he's in jail, I hope he stays in there for many years.

JOSHUA GEORGE ASBURY (12)
Paulet High School, Burton-On-Trent

THE FOLLOWER

There was a beautiful sunset upon the ocean, the waves roared over the rocks that stood on the beach. I saw something, it was hard to see what it was, it looked like a pale figure, almost floating on the sea. It became dark extremely fast, too fast as I stared at the figure. I stood, brushed myself off, then started to walk home. Owls cried in the distance. I came across a small island overflowing with trees. My heart beat fast, I glanced over and saw the same pale figure I saw before, she was staring at me.

HOLLY STINSON-SMITH (12)
Paulet High School, Burton-On-Trent

A Haunted Forest

There I was, standing outside of the most haunted castle in the whole of the world. I'd been told by many people to stay out of the castle, but I couldn't help myself. I liked horror things but this time I think they didn't want me there. Anyway, I was going in. When I got inside, I felt something there but I didn't know what. Then, I felt something behind me, I quickly turned around - there was nothing there. I got scared. I was on my own but I could hear voices. 'Help me! Please!'

Catherine Ralph (11)
Paulet High School, Burton-On-Trent

The House Next Door

It was an ordinary day for me, well that's what I thought until I heard loud bangs coming from the house next door. I ran to Mum and told her what had happened. 'It's just the wind,' she said. I woke up the next morning to more loud bangs. I put on my clothes and went to check it out. I took some chain cutters just in case. I stepped out of the front door and looked at the house. Dark and gloomy. I stepped inside. Suddenly, I felt a cold hand on my shoulder. I ran.

Jack Fotheringham (12)
Paulet High School, Burton-On-Trent

THE ROOM

I wasn't alone. The sound of footsteps dragging up the stairs, behind me the crashes of the glass against the marble floor. What was happening to me? I was hearing things. I raced to the door of the 'panic room'. I immediately slammed the door shut after me. In a few seconds, it would all be over, I knew it would. I slowly closed my eyes thinking of a place where I was safe. All of a sudden, I heard a gunshot echo outside the room. I felt my heart stop. *Bang!*

FREYA SHORTHOSE
Paulet High School, Burton-On-Trent

A DARK FIGURE

I looked behind me, there it was the dark figure. It had been following me since school. I ran faster. Suddenly, I reached a house. I ran inside and slammed the door shut. I ran upstairs and hid. There was creaking on the floorboards, then a gunshot. A baby screamed. It suddenly went silent. I went out and saw it - blood dripping on the walls spelling: 'Run'. I stood there looking, then I felt a hand on my shoulder. I screamed. It was suddenly very dark. I was dead!

MARIA JONES (11)
Paulet High School, Burton-On-Trent

ESCAPE FROM THE WOODS

In the dark woods, I see a pitch-black dress with spooky black extended hair. I hear creepy wolves coming down the hill. I don't know where they are coming from so I run back to my house. All I can see are the lights twisted off. It's like a thunderstorm has come through my house. I go into the house and shout, 'Mum! Dad!' No one answers. I shout for my sister, she doesn't answer. Everyone is out so I run upstairs. I see a face!

OLIWIA CHRZANOWSKA (12)
Paulet High School, Burton-On-Trent

DARKNESS

Darkness. Nothing but pitch-black darkness. It never ends. Never. I am alone. I think. I hope. Please say I am alone. I feel a presence but no one is here. Who am I? What is this strange place? Why am I here? How did I get here? Wait, someone or something is here. I feel a breath on the back of my neck. An icy-cold hand rests upon my shoulder. Slowly. Ever so slowly I crane my neck to see who or what is behind me. Gone, gone, I am gone...

SCARLETT DYCHE (12)
Paulet High School, Burton-On-Trent

FREAKY HOLIDAY

On a spooky day, I saw a zombie coming towards me. I was so terrified. I ran upstairs and went on my bed. I had something on my mind. I thought that there was nothing there. I looked out of the window, there was a man outside. I went downstairs and opened the door. I thought that it was a zombie. It was just a man who was lost. I let him in. He was so scared, he didn't say anything. I made him something to eat and drink. Then...

JADE FOSTER (11)
Paulet High School, Burton-On-Trent

THE UNEXPECTED JOURNEY

My head was leaning against the cold bus window, I was looking out of it, staring at someone standing in the middle of the road. How crazy! I was on my way home, on my way back from town. It started getting dark however, instead of the bus taking me home, it dropped me off at the graveyard. I took one step off the bus then, the bus drove off and left me. I was on my own. Someone ran past me. I heard a voice...

MEGAN GRIMLEY (11)
Paulet High School, Burton-On-Trent

UNTITLED

I went on holiday on a stormy night. I got there early... I got to my room. I opened the door. Suddenly, a white figure appeared. I screamed, 'Help!' I heard a massive bang! I shivered in fear. 'Who are you?' I shouted. Locks on the door clicked. I could hear footsteps, closer and closer. I felt a hand touching my shoulder. I screamed, 'Leave me alone!'
He said, 'No! I will haunt you for the rest of your life.' Suddenly, the doors opened. I walked through the door. It was pitch-black. Something touched me...

JACK POWELL (11)
Sundorne School And Sports College, Shrewsbury

THE GIRL AND THE LOST DOLL

One day there was a boy named Jeb, who was walking to school. When he got there, he noticed that there was no one in school. He opened the door and it squeaked loudly. Jeb tripped.
Jeb woke up in 1922. 'What's going on?' A doll turned its head to look at him. He felt a cold breeze through his soul. Jeb ran for his life. Suddenly, a girl appeared and screamed, 'Where is my doll?' Jeb crept down into a deep, dark cellar, his blood was pumping. As Jeb stepped forward, something bit his leg. Jeb passed out...

JOSH BOUSFIELD (11)
Sundorne School And Sports College, Shrewsbury

...

The rain swept through the park, an eerie green mist circled above the pathways, highlighted by the silver glow of the moon. The stench of death hung in the air, suffocating anything it touched. I pulled the collar of my coat closer to my face. My footsteps quickened, urgency became desperation. I needed to get out of the park, now! I felt the shadows circle around me, clawing at me, grabbing at me. Then an icy hand grabbed me. Terror took over my body. I was dead!

SAM HARRIS (11)

Sundorne School And Sports College, Shrewsbury

GOLD

The moon was shining yellow on the gold in the ship. I ran to the gold in the ship. Suddenly, I fell onto the gold. Just then, it turned to dust. I shouted, 'Noo!' I looked around and, as I did, I saw a red ruby. I crept towards the ruby in case anyone was there. I picked it up. A black figure appeared in front of me. I ran as fast as I could out of the ship and into a forest. I climbed up a tree to try and hide from the figure.

LUKE OWEN HALE (12)

Sundorne School And Sports College, Shrewsbury

In The Middle Of A Forest

In the middle of a forest, it was silent and misty, the rain poured down as the moonlight created my shadow. Suddenly, I looked and I saw a werewolf. It jumped, then I couldn't see it. I carried on and then I heard it howl. I ran...

While running, I found myself in the middle of a field. I said to my friend, 'We need to get of here!'

The next day, I woke up and my friend told me a way to get out of there...

Ernie Brown (11)

Sundorne School And Sports College, Shrewsbury

That Noise Is Here

Late at night, I went to make a cup of tea. It was very silent which was normal because I lived in the middle of nowhere. I finished my tea so I decided to go to bed. When I walked upstairs I could hear a whistling noise behind me. I started to run to my bed. I locked my door so I was safe. Suddenly, I heard the door squeaking, I dived under my quilt. I tried to see if there was anyone there. All I could see was the door, wide open...

Brandon Colin Melville (12)

Sundorne School And Sports College, Shrewsbury

FOREST

One night, I went to play with friends, suddenly, the ball went into the river and Jeff went after it. He got pulled under and we ran after him. We went into the forest, the thunder was howling like a woman with no eyes. Then, Jeff was stuck in a grave! We pulled him out and saw a portal. We went into a deep, dark forest and there were ghosts around the tree. They pushed us into a grave, I climbed out...

JACOB CASLIN

Sundorne School And Sports College, Shrewsbury

Not The Winning Story

Alex screamed as the rat scuttled across his foot. 'Chill,' said Xander from behind him in the barren woods. The rat crept towards the overgrown shrubbery.

'You chill!' boomed Alex.

'I am,' said Xander. 'Just keep on moving. We've got to be there soon!'

'Why are we even going to the abandoned hospital?'

'Because it's fun.' Alex huffed as they trudged across the marshy plain and yelped as Xander jolted him from behind. 'Argh! Why would you...?' He turned and saw half of Xander's body, the top half revealing the hole where his heart used to be...

Xander James Connor (12)

The Mary Webb School And Science College, Shrewsbury

The Shadow

One morning, four friends, Kaylah, Kieran, Taylah and Daniel were taking a stroll through the woods. All of a sudden a storm started. Clouds turned grey. They'd walked too far into the woods, they suddenly got to a creepy, horrific, abandoned house. They walked inside. Through the curtains was the shadow of someone.

'Who's that?' Taylah asked, scared.

'I don't know,' Daniel replied.

They all sprinted, they didn't realise the man was behind. A floorboard stuck up. Daniel and Kaylah fell over, not noticing. They were never seen again.

Natasha Louise Heath (12)

The Mary Webb School And Science College, Shrewsbury

THE SCARED GIRL

It was a dreadful stormy night when Jessica sheltered in the old abandoned house in the dark, ghostly forest, she was just settling in for the night. Her whole body shivered unexpectedly, she heard some creaky sounds! Suddenly, the doors started to shake rapidly. Jessica couldn't move, she was so horrified. Out of nowhere a young-looking boy appeared. Picking up courage, she whispered quietly, 'Hello, who are you?' There was no answer. She repeated herself once again but there was still no reply. She glared at him. In the blink of an eye, he disappeared.

ELISHA DAVIES (13)
The Mary Webb School And Science College, Shrewsbury

THE HOWLING WIND

Dark. Gloomy. Cold. The wind was howling like a wolf. The house had wood over the windows, there was glass all over the floor in the house. There seemed to be a ghostly figure walking along the hallway. I heard a scream, I looked around and I pictured someone jumping out at me. I tried to get out when, *bang!* The floorboard fell through. I was told everyone who entered the house never returned. Shivering. Shaking. Nervous. I'd never felt that before. Petrified. My life flashed before my eyes. It was over. I was gone. Why didn't I listen? Dead.

COURTNEY BEDDOW (14)
The Mary Webb School And Science College, Shrewsbury

THE HITCHHIKER

'Dad, when are we going to arrive at the hotel?' Oliver asked his dad. Oliver was a geeky fourteen-year-old boy with a big pair of round glasses. He was wearing brown shorts and a red polo shirt.
'We'll be there in about three hours or so,' his dad replied.
'Oh honey, that poor man is walking in the cold and the rain,' his mum said.
'Let's give him a lift.'
'Okay,' his dad replied.
Then they drove past a broken sign: 'Hitchhikers may be escaping inmates'.

GEORGE GARRETT (12)

The Mary Webb School And Science College, Shrewsbury

CHURCHYARD CHILL

It was gloomy, mysterious noises called out all around me. A colossal church with murky gravestones stood proudly in front. My palms were sweating, I had chills creeping down my spine. *Bang! Crash! Boom! What was that?* I thought, *Should I run?* I froze, with no idea of where I was. I could hear noises surrounding me as if someone was talking. The whispers floated through the air. In the distance, I could see a small figure coming towards me. It was white and gradually got brighter. The hairs on the back of my neck stood up.

DANNI VARLEY (12)

The Mary Webb School And Science College, Shrewsbury

THE ALIEN

The boy ran down the empty street. He looked around and saw an abandoned car. He ducked behind it. He looked up into the sky. The green glowing moon hung like a curtain. The white stars made an eerie glow. The boy listened for footsteps. Trying to quieten his panting breath, he prayed that it wouldn't find him. After waiting for a few minutes, the boy leapt up and ran. However, whilst looking behind him, checking for the alien, he ran into something solid, causing him to fly off his feet. There was the alien, its weapon charged.

JAMES PAYNE (13)

The Mary Webb School And Science College, Shrewsbury

LOST IN THE MAZE

There was a girl who went to a maze for fun but then she got lost. It got dark and scary. She heard a noise. When she turned around there was a terrifying scarecrow. She kept looking for the exit. She looked behind her again because she heard footsteps. This time there was a difference, there were two harrowing scarecrows! The girl ran as fast as she could but she bumped into four more scarecrows. She fell back into the bush and into another half of the maze. There were humongous spiders in that half, before she could run they...

JESSICA SHURMER (12)

The Mary Webb School And Science College, Shrewsbury

GONE

It was a cold, wet night, Helmione was walking alone on the streets of London. She kicked the water and stones along the path of the back alley until ... a black figure darted past. It was far away but close enough to hear its footsteps. It got closer until she could feel the wind on her pale face. All of a sudden she heard footsteps behind her. She slowly turned around. 'Hello? Hello? Anyone here?' No reply. She felt a cold hand on her shoulder. Were they her last words? Because from that moment nobody saw her again.

MILLIE HOLLOWAY (12)

The Mary Webb School And Science College, Shrewsbury

POLTERGEIST PIZZERIA

My first night shift. It's going to be hard staying awake. There has been death in this pizzeria but I'm getting paid. I look through the security cameras and there's three animatronics on the stage. They look menacing but I'm only working from 12am till 6am. I look up and all I see is dark nothingness. I look through the security cameras and there are only two animatronics. Weren't there three before? I look up and it is just standing there. Just staring at me. Doing absolutely nothing. Then diminishes.

RYAN ANTONY JAMES LLOYD (14)

The Mary Webb School And Science College, Shrewsbury

THE BLACK HAND

The church was a colossal mass, waiting to crumble. The dark building was built over two hundred years ago. Peter was walking past, it was raining. With a storm on its way, Peter took shelter in the church. His phone was working but had no reception. He heard glass smash. 'Hello? It's me,' Peter said. A cold, icy hand left a sooty imprint on Peter's shoulder, he froze. Then he ran towards the door but the creature got there first. He ran to the alter. The creature made its way into the light. 'Boo!'

JAMIE JONES (13)

The Mary Webb School And Science College, Shrewsbury

CINDERTHREATER

It was a cold, windy night, Cinderella was scrubbing the floor when a cold hand touched her shoulder. It turned out to be her ugly sister, saying she would not go to the ball at the palace. An evil godmother came and made Cinderella ugly. Cinderella had no idea. She went to the ball and everyone screamed and ran away. Cinderella was left alone. Then she heard a noise behind her, she ran and ran but the godmother grabbed a knife from her pocket and threw it. It went straight through Cinderella's back and into her heart.

LOIS ENTWISTLE (12)

The Mary Webb School And Science College, Shrewsbury

The Young Boy And The Bridge

It was a dark, gloomy night, you could hear the wind whistling; it felt like it was going through my body. It was like I was the only person there, I couldn't see anyone. It was like everyone had died. Suddenly, I heard footsteps, it was like someone was following me. I turned around and no one was there, so I started to walk again until I reached a horrible, cracked bridge. I walked across, I saw the bridge was slowly collapsing. I started to run, with every step I took, I was scared. Suddenly, it turned black!

Ellie-May Parker (14)

The Mary Webb School And Science College, Shrewsbury

Shadows

The forest was thick and lush with trees that danced in the breeze. As sweet, diminutive Wendy sauntered deeper into it, it seemed to be getting vaster and thicker until she couldn't find her way out. She began to panic, rushing around, when she saw a shadow fly past her. She jolted back. Nobody was there. Faster and faster she ran, getting more and more out of breath. She could run no more! That was when a hand touched her shoulder. She turned, a shadow of a girl stood, staring. 'Hello!' She disappeared!

Megan Richards (12)

The Mary Webb School And Science College, Shrewsbury

REPOSSESSED

The rain was hitting the roof like footsteps on a silent night, running down a wooden floor, echoing throughout the house. The furniture looked untouched as if the owners had just abandoned it. I snuck in, watching every move I made, examining every doorway and room. I uncovered the truth of why no one was there. They were dead! Blood was dried on the door next to where the family lay, the knife still stuck in the victim, glistening in a shaft of sunlight. Then, behind me was the sound of footsteps, running!

BILLY DAVIES (13)

The Mary Webb School And Science College, Shrewsbury

THE WORST DAY OF MY LIFE

I hate talking about the worst day of my life but I have to. It was a warm summer's evening, we had just been playing in the park. As we were leaving, we walked past the old, rickety, intimidating church, something was calling me in. I left my friends and started to trudge towards my nightmare. I felt as if something was forcing me in. Before I even touched the door, it tediously opened. I took a colossal breath and resumed walking. It was pitch-black... I felt as though I was definitely being watched...

MILLIE BATCHELOR (13)

The Mary Webb School And Science College, Shrewsbury

THE CABIN

I was lost. In the middle of the forest gloomy fog closed in, I carried on. There was a cabin, excessive rain started to fall. I decided to go in to get out of the rain. The cabin door seemed as if it only had a little life left in it. There was a few pictures of a family but the dad's face had been scratched off them. I looked about, it looked as if it had been abandoned for years. Half the windows were smashed. I phoned Sam, no answer. Suddenly, the door opened viciously behind me. 'Hello?'

BETH HEAD (12)
The Mary Webb School And Science College, Shrewsbury

THE ABANDONED HOUSE

The thunder clapped as the freezing rain dripped slowly down my spine, sending shivers through my body. There it stood, concealed in the shadows of the night, an abandoned house with its boarded up windows and cobwebbed doors. The grand oak doors screeched through the night as I opened them. Inside the house was deadly silent. All the portraits on the walls had been blacked out. As I sat in the armchair, the hairs on my neck stood up, a cold, chilled air brushed against my neck. He was there.

LUKE STEVENS (14)
The Mary Webb School And Science College, Shrewsbury

THE MAN WHO WATCHES YOU

Every night when you're asleep, a man watches you from the house next door. No one knows who he is or where he came from. We know this because a man saw him on June the 25th 2010, this is how he described him: 'He was old and grey with scars all over his face.' That's all he saw. He was reported by many people in America. One night, while you're sleeping, he will come for you. When he finds you he will kill you. So we're warning you, he will definitely find you!

ROBIN JOHN MILNER (13)

The Mary Webb School And Science College, Shrewsbury

STRANGER IN THE WOODS

The cold night air sent fearful shakes down my nervous spine. The constant crunch of the broken leaves beneath me become a noise that could disturb the dead. The repeated echoing thumping of my heart pounding against my shallow chest. The dark trapping air led me into nothing. Suddenly, a faded figure flashed before me. I snapped my neck and a ghostly scream rang in my ears. I turned my head, it was directly in front of me. Sleep took over me. My eyes opened abruptly. It was still there...

AMY MORRIS (14)

The Mary Webb School And Science College, Shrewsbury

Hide-And-Seek

I felt breathing on my back, I could hear screams. Where were my friends? It was just a game of hide-and-seek in the forest and now I was running through the forest with my eyes covered. Someone gripped my shaking hands behind my back. Where were they taking me? Sweat dripped down my face. I couldn't think, my brain was fuzzy. Footsteps got closer. The blindfold was ripped off. My eyes tried to adjust to light, it was aiming directly in my eyes. I couldn't believe what I saw...

Jess Richards (13)
The Mary Webb School And Science College, Shrewsbury

The Girl Upstairs

A young boy was walking past an old abandoned house. He heard a creaking noise so he decided to take a look. He saw nothing but then he heard a voice upstairs calling his name, 'Jack.' The boy tiptoed slowly up the broken stairs, he heard a chair creak in the bedroom, he walked in and saw someone rocking back and forth in a rocking chair. He stopped and whispered, 'Mum, is that you?' She turned around, running at him with a knife. The young boy was never seen again.

Branden Bowen (13)
The Mary Webb School And Science College, Shrewsbury

THE COLD SHOULDER

The museum was empty, or so he thought. Billy walked slowly through the museum, he had been locked in because he went into a room where he wasn't allowed. 'Ooooh!' said someone, or was it a something? The air in the museum was eerie, then he heard footsteps. 'Jack, is that you?' said Billy.
'No Billy, it's your father.'
'My father's dead,' said Billy. There was no answer. Then there was a cold hand on his shoulder.

FIN KNIGHT (14)

The Mary Webb School And Science College, Shrewsbury

BREAKING BONES

There's a forest in Transylvania, it's unspoken of. No one has ever returned. It was a dark, stormy night. I was trekking through, making sure I stayed close to the path. I always had to remember that. The mist was so thick it was like it swallowed my feet. I could hear whispers, echoing between the trees. A cold breeze sent shivers down my back and raised the hairs on my arms. Every time I stopped, it sounded like a thousand bones broke.

BENJAMIN WOOLLASTON (14)

The Mary Webb School And Science College, Shrewsbury

THE HAND

Ruby and Tom had been out for the night. They were walking home when they thought they would take a shortcut. They had to walk through a graveyard. They came across an old church that no one had been in for years. It was covered in ivy. They didn't know if they should go in or not. They decided to go in. They walked down to the front of the church. The door slammed behind them. Ruby felt a hand on her back...

SKYE DAVIES (13)

The Mary Webb School And Science College, Shrewsbury

YoungWriters
Est.1991

YOUNG WRITERS
INFORMATION

We hope you have enjoyed reading this book – and
that you will continue to in the coming years.

If you're a young writer who enjoys reading and creative writing, or the
parent of an enthusiastic poet or story writer, do visit our website
www.youngwriters.co.uk. Here you will find free
competitions, workshops and games, as well as
recommended reads, a poetry glossary and our blog.

If you would like to order further copies of this book, or any of our other
titles, then please give us a call or visit **www.youngwriters.co.uk.**

Young Writers
Remus House
Coltsfoot Drive
Peterborough
PE2 9BF
(01733) 890066 / 898110
info@youngwriters.co.uk